PRAISE FOR

TALES OF THE FROG PRINCESS

"High-spirited romantic comedy. . . . Fans of Gail Carson Levine's 'Princess Tales' should leap for it."
—*Kirkus Reviews* on *The Frog Princess*

"Quests, tests, hearts won and broken, encounters with dragons, and plenty of magic . . . As tasty as its prequel."
—*School Library Journal* on *Dragon's Breath*

"Baker's . . . vividly imagined fantasy world . . . [is] irresistible and loaded with humor."
—*VOYA* on *Once Upon a Curse*

"Kids will get a kick out of the hip *Shrek* vibe . . . in this updated fairy tale."
—*School Library Journal* on *No Place for Magic*

"An entertaining prequel. . . . An engaging main character . . . , sibling rivalries, and a romantic love interest combine in this appealing choice."
—*Booklist* on *The Salamander Spell*

BOOKS BY E. D. BAKER

Tales of the Frog Princess:
The Frog Princess
Dragon's Breath
Once Upon a Curse
No Place for Magic
The Salamander Spell
The Dragon Princess
Dragon Kiss
A Prince among Frogs
The Frog Princess Returns

———

Fairy Wings
Fairy Lies

———

Tales of the Wide-Awake Princess:
The Wide-Awake Princess
Unlocking the Spell
The Bravest Princess
Princess in Disguise
Princess between Worlds
The Princess and the Pearl
Princess Before Dawn

———

A Question of Magic

———

The Fairy-Tale Matchmaker:
The Fairy-Tale Matchmaker
The Perfect Match
The Truest Heart
The Magical Match

———

More Than a Princess

The Frog Princess Returns

E. D. BAKER

BLOOMSBURY
CHILDREN'S BOOKS
NEW YORK LONDON OXFORD NEW DELHI SYDNEY

BLOOMSBURY CHILDREN'S BOOKS
Bloomsbury Publishing Inc., part of Bloomsbury Publishing Plc
1385 Broadway, New York, NY 10018

BLOOMSBURY, BLOOMSBURY CHILDREN'S BOOKS, and the Diana logo are
trademarks of Bloomsbury Publishing Plc

First published in the United States of America in June 2017
by Bloomsbury Children's Books
Paperback edition published in June 2018

Bloomsbury books may be purchased for business or promotional use. For information
on bulk purchases please contact Macmillan Corporate and Premium Sales Department at
specialmarkets@macmillan.com

ISBN 978-1-68119-815-6 (paperback)

The Library of Congress has cataloged the hardcover edition as follows:
Names: Baker, E. D., author.
Title: The Frog Princess returns / by E. D. Baker.
Description: New York : Bloomsbury, 2017. | Series: Tales of the frog princess
Summary: Prince Eadric, having been turned from a frog
into a human again, is still in Greater Greensward where, because the
Fairy Queen has disappeared, dangerous foes are threatening, so Emma must use
her knowledge and magic to restore order.
Identifiers: LCCN 2016037699 (print) • LCCN 2016049513 (e-book)
ISBN 978-1-68119-137-9 (hardcover) • ISBN 978-1-68119-138-6 (e-book)
Subjects: | CYAC: Fairy tales. | Princesses—Fiction. | Magic—Fiction. | Characters in
literature—Fiction. | BISAC: JUVENILE FICTION/Fantasy & Magic. | JUVENILE
FICTION/ Fairy Tales & Folklore/General. | JUVENILE FICTION/Love & Romance.
Classification: LCC PZ8.B173 Fro 2017 (print) | LCC PZ8.B173 (e-book) | DDC [Fic]—dc23
LC record available at https://lccn.loc.gov/2016037699

Typeset by Westchester Publishing Services
Printed and bound in the U.S.A. by Berryville Graphics Inc., Berryville, Virginia
2 4 6 8 10 9 7 5 3 1

All papers used by Bloomsbury Publishing Plc are natural, recyclable products
made from wood grown in well-managed forests. The manufacturing processes
conform to the environmental regulations of the country of origin.

To find out more about our authors and books visit www.bloomsbury.com
and sign up for our newsletters.

I dedicate this book to all my loyal fans who have asked for more tales of the Frog Princess

The
Frog Princess
Returns

"With this gift comes greater power as well as greater responsibility, for the Green Witch must be the kingdom's protector, using her magic to ensure the safety of its inhabitants, whether human- or fairy-kind."

—The Fairy Queen as she bestowed the title and ring on the first Green Witch

One

"*D*o we *have* to be sharks, Emma?" Eadric asked as I took his hand in mine.

We were standing at the edge of the moat, preparing to go monster-hunting. My aunt Grassina had put countless monsters in the moat while under the family curse. For centuries, all the girls in our family had turned nasty if they touched a flower after their sixteenth birthday. With the possibility that I might fall prey to the curse, I had refused to marry Eadric unless we could end it. Eadric and I had gone back in time to try to keep an angry fairy from saying the curse. Although we hadn't been successful, we had learned a great deal, including the original wording. It wasn't until my grandfather kissed my grandmother that the curse was finally over. Suddenly nice again, Grassina was busy trying to get her life back in order while I tried to clean up the mess she'd made.

"I sent away the smaller monsters," I told Eadric. "Now

all that's left are the truly awful ones. I have to see them for my spell to work, so we need to go into the moat to find them. If we're going to do this, we have to be even worse than the monsters. I told you about the time Grassina was floating on the moat in a bubble and how she fell in when the bubble popped. A really horrible monster went after her, so she turned herself into an enormous shark that frightened the monster. If being a shark worked for her, it should work for us, too. You don't have to go if you'd rather stay here and watch."

"Oh, no! I'm going," said Eadric. "There's no way I'd let you hunt monsters without me. I just thought it might be more fun if we were monsters, too. But if you think we should be sharks, make me the biggest and nastiest shark ever!"

"I'll try," I said, and started to recite the spell.

> Curved fin circling round and round,
> Cold eyes ever hunting,
> Moving close without a sound,
> Rows of sharp teeth glinting.
>
> Now we'll each become a shark
> Much bigger than our prey.
> We'll make the monsters flee the dark
> And want to go away.

I had scarcely said the last few words when Eadric and I began to change. I dropped his hand as my fingers fused together and my arms became fins. My eyes moved to the top of my head, which became long and pointed. I could feel my teeth shift, and suddenly I had far too many in my mouth.

Eadric flopped to the ground as his legs became fused. He fell into the water first. I joined him seconds later. We finished our transformations in the murky water of the moat, our gills fluttering as we took our first breaths as sharks.

We had never turned into sharks before, so it took some time to learn how to swim this way. Eadric was bigger than me, and I had to get out of his way as he floundered around, wallowing from side to side. I mastered the knack of swimming before he did, but he soon caught on and shot past me under the drawbridge, where I could see a monster lurking in the shadows.

The monster resembled a long snake with sharp ridges along its back and sides. Skinny arms with wicked-looking claws grew from its body at irregular intervals. I probably wouldn't have seen the monster at all if worm-like lines that glowed in the dark hadn't decorated its body. I suppose they might have attracted other monsters, but all it did for me was make the monster easier to spot. Eadric went for it as if he wanted to fight, but I had something else in mind. Looking straight at the monster, I said,

Monster swimming in the moat,
It's time for you to go.
Find a new home far away,
A place no man can know.

Eadric was grappling with the monster when my spell took effect. I held my breath, afraid that the monster might hurt my beloved, but I didn't need to worry. One moment the monster was wrapped around Eadric, scraping at his tough hide with its claws, the next the monster was gone, leaving the biggest shark I had ever seen chomping at the water that had rushed in to fill the void.

"That was fun!" Eadric said, giving me a very toothy grin.

"We're not here to fight them," I told him. "I just want to find them so I can send them away."

"But I have to protect you until you say the whole spell," he said. "And I have to keep them from swimming off so you can still see them, right?"

I sighed. "I suppose so," I said. "But . . ."

Eadric was off looking for another monster before I could say any more. He was surprisingly good at finding monsters, even those half buried in the mud. We searched the entire moat, going full circle around the castle, discovering more monsters than I had expected. Some tried to attack us as we drew close, while others fled at the sight of two big sharks. We saw one armored in a turtle-like shell with snapping heads at every opening. Another was shaped like a ball with powerful tentacles attached to it every few inches. The most frightening looked innocent enough at first. It was shaped like an ordinary fish except for the spiky frill around its neck. I wasn't even sure it was a monster until it came upon a small fish and the frill contracted, shooting a poisoned spine into its victim. When the poor fish thrashed as if in terrible pain, I hurried to recite the spell without going any closer.

We thought we had found all our quarry, until we came across a nest of baby monsters. Seeing us, the little blobs of eyeball-filled jelly sped away, making high-pitched shrieking sounds like air escaping from an inflated balloon. I remembered seeing the adult version of this monster months ago. It had been much bigger and a lot slower. When I chased the babies, they were too squishy to hold on to and even harder for sharks to corral. I was wondering if we should try to chase down all the babies and send them away at once, or try to take care of them individually, when a rock hit me on the nose. Startled, I glanced at the rock as it fell to the bottom of the moat. The words *I need to talk to you. Please come up!* were written in glowing letters.

Spinning around, I looked toward the bank and saw a full-sized fairy looking down at me. Her orange, yellow, and red hair was vibrant and beautiful, but it was her worried expression that drew me to her.

"Eadric, we need to get out now," I told him as three baby monsters streaked past. "Someone wants to talk to me. We'll have to come back to catch the babies, but I won't be able to do it without a new spell and a very big net."

Eadric peered up at the fairy. "Who is it?"

"I don't know," I said, swimming toward the edge of the moat, "but it must be important enough for her to throw a rock at me. If it isn't, I'm not going to be happy."

Reaching the bank, we realized that we couldn't get out of the water while we were sharks. This meant that I had to change us back while we were still in the moat. The spell took only seconds. Eadric soon heaved himself onto dry land, but my gown weighed me down, making it that much harder. I was struggling to climb out when Eadric reached for my hand and pulled me up as if I didn't weigh anything at all.

"Sorry about that," the fairy said, looking contrite. "I didn't mean to hit you with the rock. I just wanted to get your attention. You see, the leaves on my trees are wilting and nothing I do is making them better. I didn't know where to turn until I heard that you're supposed to help fairies in need. You are the Green Witch, aren't you?"

I nodded and wiped the water from my eyes. "And your name is . . . ?"

"Oh, sorry! I'm Maple, and my trees are maples, of course. Mine aren't the only trees that are sick. I've heard

8

that there are others in the enchanted forest that are also doing poorly."

"I'm afraid I don't know much about trees," I told her. "Perhaps you should talk to my aunt Grassina. She knows a lot about plants. Maybe she can help you. This morning she said she was going into the swamp with her fiancé, Haywood. You might be able to find her there."

"I'll go see her right now. Thank you!" said Maple. A moment later, she had made herself small and was flying in the direction of the swamp.

Although we couldn't see the drawbridge from where we stood, we could hear the thunder of hooves crossing it and a carriage rattling behind. "Who do you think that is?" Eadric asked. "It has the same creak as my parents' carriage."

"We weren't expecting anyone today," I said as we both started walking.

We reached the point where we could see the draw-bridge just as the carriage disappeared beyond the gate. "That looked like my parents' carriage," said Eadric. "I wonder why they came back so soon. Do you suppose there's something wrong? I hope nothing terrible has happened in Upper Montevista. Maybe Bradston has done something dumb and gotten hurt."

I was afraid that it was something else entirely. King Bodamin, Queen Frazzela, and their younger son, Bradston, had left only two weeks before, after a very short visit. They had come for my birthday tournament and left when they learned that most of the women in my family were witches, myself included. The queen hated witches, and the fact that her older son had fallen in love with one was more than she could handle. Both the king and queen had been upset that Eadric had refused to go with them when they left. I was afraid that they had decided to try to force him to come home.

"I'm sure they're fine," I said, not wanting to tell him what was worrying me. "We'll have to get cleaned up before we see them. Perhaps we should wait until we're sure they've gone inside."

Eadric shook his head. "It might be urgent. The sooner I see them, the sooner I'll know that everything is all right."

"Then at least let me dry us off," I said. The spell I used was short but effective. Although it dried our clothes and hair, it left everything as dirty as before. I would have used a cleaning spell next, but Eadric was already hurrying across the drawbridge.

I sighed as I followed him. Eadric was probably right. It was better to find out what was really going on than to make ourselves sick worrying.

I was still hoping that everyone had gone inside and that I could change my clothes before I saw them when my mother's voice rang out. "There they are! Emma,

Eadric, come meet Princess Adara. Apparently she's a long-lost cousin that we didn't even know we had. Isn't that delightful?"

I looked up and saw my mother standing on the castle steps with a stranger beside her. The princess was a beautiful girl about my own age. She had long blond hair that was so pale it was almost white and vivid blue eyes that tilted at the corners. After sparing me only the briefest of glances, she turned to Eadric and smiled, making her even lovelier. Standing there with dirty hands and face and soiled clothes that smelled like the moat, I suddenly felt very self-conscious.

When I glanced at Eadric and saw the expression on his face, I had to bite my tongue so I wouldn't snap at him. He was wearing the same look he'd worn when he saw the mermaids in Coral's castle. It was the same look he'd had when he'd met Hazel, the first Green Witch. I'd hated that look and had hoped I'd never see it again.

"Adara, this is my daughter, Emma," my mother said as Eadric and I approached the steps. "And this is Prince Eadric."

"Hello, Emma," Adara said without looking my way. Her tone was much warmer when she smiled at Eadric and said, "Hello, Eadric! I really like your name. It makes me think of someone who's strong, yet sensitive; someone I'd really like to get to know better."

I made a strangled sound, not wanting to be ill in front

11

of everyone, but Eadric seemed to like her. "You're very perceptive," he said and smiled.

"Emma and Eadric plan to get married as soon as possible," my mother announced in an overly loud voice.

I glanced at my mother. She knew that Eadric and I had yet to set a date, but when she looked at me and our eyes met, I understood right away. Princess Adara was far prettier than me and therefore a threat in my mother's eyes. When I turned to Eadric and saw that that look was still on his face, I wondered if she was right.

"How nice," Adara said, her gaze never leaving Eadric.

"Adara was visiting Eadric's parents when she mentioned that she was related to us, but had never actually visited Greater Greensward," my mother continued. "Queen Frazzela thought we might like to meet our cousin and offered the use of her carriage. Wasn't that nice of her?"

I noticed the edge in my mother's voice, but I doubted either Adara or Eadric did. Eadric was still looking dazed, while Adara looked like a hungry cat that had just spotted a bowl of fresh cream. It was a look I *really* didn't like.

Two

"I think I should introduce you to my husband, King Limelyn," said my mother, linking her arm with Adara's.

"Are you going, too?" Adara asked Eadric.

"I suppose so," he replied.

"Then I'd love to meet the king!" said Adara, and let my mother lead her into the castle. Eadric fell into step right behind her, following like a puppy on a leash.

"I guess we're all going," I said through gritted teeth as I walked beside him, silently fuming.

My father and a group of his knights were talking in the far corner of the Hall. Mother headed straight for him, taking Adara with her. The princess kept glancing back at Eadric, which was enough to make him follow. Although I had many other things to attend to, keeping an eye on Adara felt like the most important.

When two of the knights excused themselves and walked away, my father was left with Sir Ranulf, Sir Nerigen, and Sir Geoffrey. Sir Ranulf was the youngest and handsomest knight in the castle. All the ladies-in-waiting professed to be in love with him, and more than one serving girl had fainted when he looked her way. Even so, Adara scarcely spared him a glance. My darling Eadric was handsome in my eyes, but even I knew that most people considered him almost plain. Adara, however, couldn't seem to take her eyes off him.

"Limelyn," my mother said, "I want you to meet Princess Adara. She's from . . . What is the name of your kingdom again, dear?"

"I'm from Lower Mucksworthy," said the princess. "It's just north of Soggy Molvinia, Your Majesty."

"I'm familiar with the kingdom," said the king. "Welcome to Greater Greensward, Adara."

"The princess claims to be a relative of ours," the queen continued. "Although I'm not quite sure of the connection. Perhaps you can explain it to me again, Adara. You said you were a cousin, but I'm still not sure how we're related."

Adara smiled sweetly at my mother. "I'm a cousin a number of times removed, but I really can't say how many. I'm terrible at figuring out that kind of thing."

Mother's look wasn't exactly warm. "It sounds as if you're a distant relative—if that," she added under her breath.

"How long will you be staying with us?" asked my father.

"As long as you'll have me," said Adara. "I'm in no hurry to get home. I have six brothers and four sisters. I love my family, but it's nice to get away for a while. What about you, Eadric? Do you want a big family someday?"

"Uh . . . ," Eadric said, looking confused.

"Hello, everyone!" my grandmother called out as she entered the Great Hall. "It's so nice to find you all together."

My grandmother Olivene lived at the Old Witches' Retirement Community, but she often came to the castle to visit. Although her husband had died years before, his ghost still claimed a room in the dungeon. They missed each other terribly when they were apart.

"Good day, Mother," said the queen. "Come meet our guest. Mother, this is Princess Adara from . . ."

"Lower Mucksworthy," said the princess after a quick glance at my mother.

I could tell that my mother didn't like the girl and was pretending to forget the name of her kingdom on purpose. I was wondering if Adara could tell, too.

"Adara, this is dowager Queen Olivene," my mother said. "Mother, Princess Adara claims to be a relative of ours."

My grandmother raised one eyebrow. "Oh? How marvelous! Would you mind explaining this familial connection? I find such things fascinating!"

Adara smiled and nodded. "It's quite simple, really. My great-grandfather King Snodgrass was married to a princess from Greater Greensward. I believe her name was Ermingarde."

"Ah, yes! Ermingarde was my great-great-aunt," said Grandmother. "I understand she was very lovely."

"Her portrait hangs in our Great Hall. I've been told I look just like her," Adara said, looking pleased with herself.

"How charming!" Grandmother declared. "I believe I have a small portrait of her myself. I never expected to see her likeness in real life!"

For some reason, this seemed to make Adara uncomfortable, and made my grandmother smile.

"Queen Olivene collects such things," my mother explained. "The old portraits were stored in the dungeon until I had it cleaned out. She took them all and cleaned them for us so they're all as good as new."

"Indeed," said Grandmother. "I'm afraid I must ask you to excuse me now. I have some urgent business to attend to. Emma, I'll need your help with this."

"But I was just...," I began, then saw the look on Grandmother's face. Whatever she needed me for, there was no getting out of it.

I glanced at Adara one last time before leaving the Hall. She was looking at Eadric from under her lashes, which seemed to make him nervous.

Grandmother led the way down the corridor to a quiet room where we could talk. "I think that girl is a little liar," she told me once the door was closed. "That portrait is one of my favorites, and I know exactly what Ermingarde looked like. She had red hair like yours and was missing a front tooth from when she fell off a swing as a child. No one ever called her a beauty. I've kept all the family records I've come across over the years. I'm going to dig through them and see what I can find. In the meantime, don't trust Adara. She has her eye on your Eadric. It's easy to see that she means to get him for herself. But don't worry. Our family will take care of the girl. I know just what to do to give her a *special* welcome. She'll be gone before you know it."

Grandmother started from the room wearing a determined look. Curious, I was following her to ask what she had planned, but a pink-haired fairy wearing a gown of water lily petals stopped me just outside the door.

"Are you the Green Witch?" she asked, planting herself in front of me. "Because if you are, I need your help."

I nodded, still thinking about Adara and Eadric and what Grandmother had in mind. "I am. The Green Witch, I mean."

"And I'm Water Lily," said the fairy. "The pond where my lilies grow is drying up. The springs that feed it haven't given me a drop of water in weeks. If I don't get water soon, my roots will be exposed! Is there anything you can do?"

"We've had plenty of rain," I told her, wishing she hadn't stopped me. I really wanted to talk to Grandmother before she did whatever she had planned.

"I know, but it hasn't made much difference," the fairy replied.

"I'll come see you as soon as I can, but first I want to do a little research. In the meantime, ask around and see if this is happening to anyone else. I need to know if this is widespread or an isolated incident."

"I will!" said the fairy. "I'll ask everyone in my neighborhood!"

Three

When I returned to the Great Hall, Eadric was talking to my father's knights about going outside for jousting practice. My hopes that Adara would find this boring and not want to go were dashed when she perked up and said, "I love jousting! I can't wait to see you practice! Are you going to hold a tournament soon?"

"My father held one to celebrate my birthday a few weeks ago," I told her. "I doubt we'll hold another for a very long time."

The tournament had been a way to get Eadric's parents to visit so my parents could meet them. Because of the magical mishaps and the subsequent early departure of King Bodamin and Queen Frazzela, I was sure it would be many years before we held another tournament in Greater Greensward. Eadric still liked to practice, however, because the same skills used in jousting were often used in real combat.

"Oh," Adara said, sounding disappointed. After a

moment's thought, she seemed to brighten. "Maybe we can change the king's mind!" Hooking her arm through Eadric's, she walked beside him to the door. Eadric glanced back at me, wearing a desperate look. Taking pity on him, I took his other arm and gave it a squeeze as we walked down the corridor. Because the doorway to the courtyard wasn't wide enough for three people to walk side by side, Eadric removed his arm from Adara's with a murmured apology and walked through holding on to me. When I glanced at Adara, she looked annoyed, but her expression turned into a smile when she saw me looking her way.

Eadric's stallion, Bright Country, was saddled and ready by the time we walked around the outside of the castle. The horses belonging to the other knights were also there, but only Bright Country seemed happy to see his owner.

Adara and I watched Eadric and the knights take turns charging at the quintain. Eadric was one of the best, but I couldn't help remembering how he could have been killed at the tournament when Prince Jorge had used a sharpened lance. I was relieved when they finished practice and Eadric handed Bright Country's reins over to a stable boy.

"I need to do some research," I told Eadric as we were walking back to the castle.

"Sounds good to me," he said, yawning. "I could use a nap."

Eadric had gotten in the habit of joining me in my tower when I worked. He found my window seat very comfortable and often took a nap on it. I enjoyed his company even when we didn't talk.

Adara always seemed to listen in on our conversations, so I was sure that she knew we were going to be occupied. Even so, she followed us up the spiral stairs to my rooms at the top of the tower.

I went to work right away, taking out the parchments and books that I thought might hold information about withered trees or dried-up springs. Eadric had already started to stretch out on the window seat when Adara sat down next to him, forcing him to sit up. Adara moved closer, making him scoot sideways. Each time he tried to put space between them, she inched closer, until he was wedged against the wall that flanked the window seat. Scowling, he jumped to his feet and walked a few steps.

Adara's gaze never left Eadric. "What's your favorite food? Is it eels? Your mother says that your father loves eels, but I don't care for them myself. They make me break out in a terrible rash. Does anything make you break out in a rash?"

"Not really," said Eadric.

"Who was the first girl you kissed? Was it Emma? Are you a good kisser?"

"Uh," said Eadric.

"Do you wear a nightshirt when you sleep? I've heard that some men don't."

Eadric looked stunned and didn't say anything.

"Do you snore? I don't mind if you do. My father snores every night. I can hear him all the way in my room, which isn't anywhere near his. He sounds like a bull snorting in his pen."

When I glanced at Eadric, I could tell that he was becoming increasingly annoyed and uncomfortable. Her chatter was annoying me, too, and I found it really hard to concentrate. I was trying to think of something polite that I could say to get her to leave when a sparrow flew through the window just over Adara's head, carrying a slip of parchment.

When Adara let out a small shriek and jumped to her feet, Eadric took advantage of her absence and lay down, claiming the window seat for himself. The sparrow brought the parchment to me, dropping it on my desk before flying out the window.

My grandmother had sent me a note.

Come down to the Great Hall. I'm holding an impromptu party. Bring Eadric and that princess!

"Eadric," I said as I rolled up the parchment I'd been studying. "You need to get up. Grandmother has invited us to a party. Apparently, it's starting now."

"What? She's never had a party before," Eadric said and got to his feet.

"Perhaps it's in my honor," Adara said, looking smug.

"Maybe," I said, wondering if this was part of grandmother's plan to get rid of her.

❧

I wasn't sure what to expect when we went downstairs, but I would never have expected what we actually found. My grandmother had invited all her friends from the Old Witches' Retirement Community, and quite a few of them had come. Grandmother had lived there for many years; she'd been under the family curse for most of that time. I had broken the curse the day of my birthday party, so she was no longer horrible. Her friends, however, were horrible without a curse, and not people I'd ever want to spend time with for very long.

The noise was deafening when we entered the Hall, and it looked as if prisoners from a very nasty dungeon were rioting. There were witches of every description: tall, short, fat, thin, young, old, dressed in rags, or the epitome of elegance. The only thing that they seemed to have in common was that they were all witches.

Frightened-looking serving girls stood behind a long table at one end of the hall, serving mugs of cider and bite-sized pieces of food. A few of the witches were actually drinking the cider, but the rest were drinking some smelly green stuff that they had brought with them. There was music, although no actual musicians, and the stench of perspiring bodies was nearly overpowering.

I was glad that my parents weren't there. They would have been appalled to see witches dancing on the tables with their skirts hiked up to their knees, and to see others casting spells on each other, giving their friends snuffling pig snouts and wagging dog tails. Even my grandmother looked slightly uncomfortable, until she saw Adara walk into the room. Her face lit up then, and she walked toward us, saying, "I'm so glad that you could come."

Taking Adara by the hand, she led her farther into the room. "I want you to meet my friends. Ladies, this is Princess Adara from Lower Mucksworthy. She's our guest and I want you to treat her accordingly."

"Come with me, Princess," a skinny woman with a beak-like nose called out, grabbing Adara by the elbow. With the help of some other women, they hefted her onto a table and jumped up to dance beside her.

"That's not the way we usually treat guests," Eadric shouted into my ear.

"I know," I shouted back. "Grandmother has decided that Adara deserves special treatment."

While Eadric and I sat on the sidelines, the witches made Adara dance until she could barely stand. "Is she dancing because she wants to or because your friends cast a spell on her?" I finally asked my grandmother.

"Does it matter?" Grandmother said with a shrug. "She seems to be enjoying it."

"Is this your plan to make Adara want to leave?" I asked, gesturing to encompass the entire Hall and all the witches.

My grandmother laughed and shook her head. "It would be nice if this was all it took, but this is only part of what I have in mind. Just wait. You'll see."

When they finally took a break, the witches handed Adara a mug of the green drink. She took a small sip, made an awful face, and passed it to the witch next to her, who gladly chugged it down. They started dancing again then, as wildly as before. I saw the princess looking toward Eadric more than once, but every time she tried to leave, the witches pulled her back into their merrymaking.

"Contest time!" shouted a stout witch with a wart-covered nose. "What will it be this week?"

"Grossest food!" shouted a witch.

"How about ugliest face!" yelled another.

"You'd win that hands down without even trying, Turinna!" shouted a tall witch with the biggest stick-out ears I'd ever seen. "Think of something harder!"

"Stinkiest feet!" a hoarse voice suggested. Everyone laughed, but then they all agreed that it sounded like the best idea.

"And our new guest can be the judge!" hollered the tall, thin witch.

I glanced at Adara, who turned pale when the other witches agreed.

"Everybody, sit on the benches and take off your shoes and socks," ordered the skinny witch. "Princess, come with me! You have lots of sniffing to do!"

Rushing to the benches, the witches pushed and shoved until they all had seats. A lot of elbow-jabbing and name-calling followed as they took off their shoes and socks. Suddenly the Great Hall smelled like rotting cheese and something dead that one of the dogs might have dragged in.

Adara looked sick as the skinny witch dragged her down the line, making her stop to take a deep breath next to each and every witch. After a while, Adara's face was slightly green, but it wasn't until she stood before an older witch with stringy hair and soiled clothes that she made a soft sound and fainted.

"We have our winner!" shouted the skinny witch, and the rest began to cheer. Two witches jumped up from their seats. After rolling Adara onto her back, they set their shoes and socks on her stomach. One grabbed her hands and the other grabbed her legs so they could carry her over to us. She was coming around when they dropped her on the floor.

"Good little princess!" one said, patting Adara on the

head before walking to a nearby bench to put her socks and shoes on again.

Eadric had his hand over his mouth, trying not to laugh. I shook my head and helped Adara to her feet. "That must have been truly awful," I said, expecting her to agree.

"No more than I'd expect from a place like this," she replied, quenching even the tiniest hint of sympathy I might have felt.

The party wound down about an hour later. A number of witches had already gone home when Adara was finally able to escape from the Great Hall, looking tired and disheveled. For the first time since she'd arrived, she came over to talk to me. "I've never danced so much in my life! Could you tell me where I'll be sleeping tonight? I need to rest for a little while."

I sent for the steward, who escorted Adara to her room. Eadric and I were happy to spend the rest of the afternoon in my tower, doing what we had tried to do before. I found some books about trees, and one that mentioned dried-up springs, but nothing that could actually help. Eadric took his nap on my window seat, snoring softly.

The shadows were lengthening in the room when I finally looked up from my studies. It was time to get ready for supper. Leaving Eadric still sleeping, I went through the door into my bedchamber. The water in the basin was cold, so I said a quick spell to warm it before washing my face and hands. After changing into a nicer gown and brushing my hair until it shone, I returned to my workroom, where Eadric was sitting up, looking groggy. His hair was flattened on one side and he had a crease in his cheek from the cushion, but I thought he looked very sweet.

When he saw me, he patted the window seat, saying, "Can you sit with me? There's something I wanted to talk to you about."

I nodded and took a seat, turning to look into his eyes.

"Ever since we met that girl, she hasn't left me alone," he said, frowning.

"Yes, I know," I replied.

"She keeps pestering me and it's really annoying."

"Yes, I know," I said again.

"There's only one girl for me," he said, pulling me into his arms.

"Yes, I know," I whispered.

"You know that I love you with all my heart, right?" I would have answered, but then he kissed me.

Suddenly someone was pounding on the door. We pulled apart and turned to the door, but before we could answer, it opened and Adara walked in.

"I have got to renew the 'keep out' spell on that door," I muttered to myself.

"It's almost supper time. Aren't you going to the Great Hall to eat?" asked Adara.

"Yes, we are!" Eadric and I both said, then turned to smile as we looked into each other's eyes.

Four

The Great Hall was already crowded when we walked in the door. I was surprised to see that my grandmother was still there, because she usually didn't stay for supper. My aunt Grassina was sitting beside Haywood. Three empty chairs had been left between my father and Grassina; enough for Eadric, Adara, and me. Eadric took his usual seat beside my father, but when I went to my seat, Adara pushed past me and sat there instead.

Eadric frowned, saying, "I'm sorry, but Emma always sits there."

"I'm sure she won't mind if I do," said Adara. "I'm your guest. In my kingdom, the guests always get the best of everything!"

I must have looked unhappy when I took the seat between Adara and Grassina, because my aunt patted my hand. "Don't worry," she said in a soft voice. "Olivene told us everything. Leave it to us."

Adara had turned her back to me so she was facing Eadric and didn't notice Grassina flick her fingers. The front legs of the chair Adara was sitting on abruptly lost two inches and dropped with a loud *thunk*. Adara slid forward and would have fallen to the floor if the table hadn't stopped her.

"What was that?" she asked, pushing herself farther back on the seat.

"What was what?" I said, and reached for my mug of cider. I was sipping my drink when the roast boar was set on the table in front of Adara. I thought this was odd, because my parents were usually served first, but no one else seemed to notice.

"It looks delicious and smells even better!" Adara declared. "I want the apple and the choicest cut of meat!"

I felt my aunt stirring beside me. A moment later, the roasted pig rolled its eyes and spit the apple onto Adara's trencher. The princess gasped and pushed her chair back. Grassina flicked her fingers again and the back legs of the chair lost three inches, making it lower than the front. When Adara pushed again, the chair toppled over backward, crashing to the floor.

All the men at the table jumped to their feet. "Are you all right?" asked Eadric as he helped her up.

"I'm fine," she said, clinging to him like a limpet. "Did you see what the pig just did?"

31

"What pig?" he asked as he detached her arms from around his waist and set her chair upright. Somehow the chair seemed to be its normal height when he touched it. "Do you mean the roasted boar?"

I glanced at the platter holding the boar. The apple was back in its mouth and it was staring fixedly ahead.

"I just . . . I saw . . . Never mind," Adara said.

She seemed a little shaky when she sat down again. The chair immediately became shorter, although the legs were even again. The top of the table came up to her chest, making it hard to reach her trencher. She looked up at me and frowned. "Did you do something to this chair? Queen Frazzela said that you're a witch."

"I am indeed, but I didn't do anything to that chair," I told her. "Why, what's wrong with it?"

Adara scowled at me. "I know you did this!"

"Did what?" said Grassina.

"Nothing," Adara said. She glanced around as if expecting something else to happen. When nothing did, she reached for her mug of cider. Raising it to her lips, she tilted the mug. Cider dribbled down her chin and across the front of her gown. I thought it looked like there was a hole in the mug, but when she looked at it, there wasn't anything wrong.

Eadric shook his head and handed her his napkin as she inspected her gown.

When I peeked at Grassina, she was trying not to laugh.

32

A hound bumped into my leg and I glanced down. My father's hounds were trained to stay away from the tables when we were eating, but they were here now, begging for food. When I saw my father surreptitiously toss a scrap of meat under Adara's chair, I knew that he was in on Olivene's plan, too.

Seeing the meat, the hounds scampered under the table, pushing and growling as they tried to reach it first. Within seconds, Adara was surrounded by big, slobbering dogs. "Get them away from me!" she cried as the dogs bumped into her and stepped on her feet.

I pulled my legs out of the way as the dogs got rougher. Eadric started to stand up as if he was about to intervene, but my father tapped him on the shoulder and shook his head. Eadric looked puzzled when he sat down again. A fight nearly broke out between the hounds when one nipped another, but then Bowser, my father's biggest hound, snapped up the meat and ran off, nearly knocking Adara over again.

Two serving girls brought a huge tureen of eel stew to the table. When they offered it to us, I looked into the tureen at the same time as Adara. The eels were swimming around, gliding over one another in loose and slippery knots. Grimacing, Adara shook her head and waved the serving girls off.

They carried the stew down the table, offering it to Grassina and Haywood, her betrothed. Although my aunt declined the stew, Haywood made little chirruping sounds and said, "Yes! Lots, please!"

I noticed that the eels were limp and looked quite cooked when one of the girls ladled stew into a bowl for Haywood. Adara was watching when Haywood stuck his face in the bowl and began to devour the eels just as he would have when he was an enchanted otter. He had been working on giving up his otter-like ways ever since Grassina turned him back, but it seemed he had reverted, at least for tonight. Making loud slurping sounds, he ate every bit of the stew and licked the bowl clean. When he was done, he wiped the bowl with his fingers and licked them clean as well.

I heard gagging sounds behind me. Apparently, Adara had never seen a former otter eat.

"I spoke to that fairy Maple," Grassina told me. "She described what was happening to her trees. Haywood and I went to take a look, but everything seemed normal to us, aside from the leaves withering, of course. I didn't see any sign of blight or an insect infestation, and the surrounding plants seemed healthy, so it wasn't lack of water. I'm sorry, but I couldn't help her."

"Thank you for trying," I said. "I looked through all my books and parchments, but I couldn't find anything, either."

"Oh, good, here's dessert," said Grassina. "It looks like gooseberry pie."

"But I've hardly eaten anything yet!" Adara wailed.

"You are a slow eater," Haywood told her. "I've had three helpings already. Maybe part of your problem is your posture. You really should sit up when you eat. Slouching like that can't be good for the digestion."

"I'm not slouching!" cried Adara. "My chair got shorter."

"Uh-huh," he said as if he didn't believe her.

"Emma," my mother said from farther down the table. "Why don't you and Eadric go see your grandfather after supper? Mother tells me that you haven't visited him lately."

"We really should," I said, looking past Adara to Eadric. "It has been a while. And I have a question that I want to ask him."

"Sounds good to me," Eadric said. "I really like your grandfather. He tells the best stories! But first I need a slice of that gooseberry pie. I might even have to eat two!"

❧

When Eadric finally declared that he'd had enough to eat, we excused ourselves and started to leave the dais, where the royal family was seated. Everyone was watching when Adara hurried after us. I doubted she was going to make any friends in the castle. Everyone liked Eadric and was glad that he was marrying into the family. Adara's single-minded pursuit of the man I meant to marry was enough to turn them all against her.

The princess didn't question where we were going until we started down the stairs to the dungeon, walking single file. "Why are we going down here, Emma? I thought your grandfather must be upstairs, sick in bed."

"He stays down here," said Eadric, who was carrying a torch in case the ones in the dungeon had gone out. "You don't have to come if you don't want to. It is cold where we're going."

"I don't mind the cold," Adara told him, forcing a smile.

When we reached the bottom of the stairs, most of the torches on the walls were lit, but their light was feeble and their flames wavered and flickered as if unseen people were passing by. Eadric and I were used to this, but Adara started to look over her shoulder and into the deeper shadows as we walked down the corridor. I went first because I was better able to handle anything we might encounter. Eadric came next, holding the torch high so it illuminated more of the corridor. When I looked back, Adara was walking so close to Eadric that she was almost stepping on his heels. She was pale and her eyes were darting everywhere. Even so, she didn't say a word.

Although I had been working to clean up the errant magic that had gotten worse while Grassina lived in the dungeon, there was still enough around to keep us from getting too complacent. We were fortunate that we encountered only one patch of magic mist. The moment it reached us, the mist made us look fifty years older.

"What just happened?" cried Adara. "You two look so old now. And my hands! They look like my great-aunt Maude's! What have you done to me?"

"Keep walking," I told her.

We had scarcely taken three steps when we left the mist and looked young again.

"Thank goodness," Adara said, pressing her hands to her cheeks. "That was truly horrible!"

A few ghosts drifted out one wall and through another as we walked past, but they were going about their own affairs and were too busy to talk to us. I heard Adara make a small, strangled kind of sound, but she didn't say anything.

We had just turned down another corridor when there was a loud *crash!* and the wall beside us crumbled. Moat water gushed in, rushing past us and rising higher and higher in the narrow corridor. Although I could see and hear the water, I couldn't feel it, and the torches that were now underwater didn't go out.

"We have to get out of here!" cried Adara as she pulled on Eadric's arm.

"Not yet," Eadric told her. "I want to see this part."

Footsteps thudded back the way we had come. Soon I heard splashing, and the castle's soldiers came into view. The water level was already going down, so the men had to swim for only a short time. They were slogging through knee-deep water when I noticed that they wore old-fashioned bucket-like helmets and poorly-stitched-together leather for armor.

"Who are these people?" asked Adara.

"Just watch," said Eadric.

I turned back to the wall in time to see men from the invading army pour through the gaping hole. After the first clash of soldiers, fighting began in earnest. I backed up as the fighting drew closer. When it was all around us, I happened to glance at Adara. Terror stricken, she was clinging to Eadric, who was too intent on the swordplay to notice the girl beside him. A sound behind me made me look back just as a soldier slashed at his opponent. The sword cut off the man's head and would have cut off mine as well if the combatants had been flesh and bone. It was a good effect, and I would have to tell the ghosts what I thought. After much hard work, their reenactments seemed very realistic.

As the soldiers carried the fighting out of sight around the corner, I turned toward Eadric. "What did you think?" I asked. "I thought they did a very good job this time."

"That wasn't real?" Adara asked, her voice coming out in a squeak.

Eadric looked surprised. "You thought it was real? Didn't you see their armor and the weapons they were using? That battle took place hundreds of years ago! I'd forgotten that this was the week they were going to reen-act the Battle of the Two-Month Siege. We learn about it in Upper Montevista. Of course, my ancestors were lead-ing the invading army."

"I thought we were about to be killed!" Adara cried.

"The ghosts couldn't hurt you if they wanted to," Ead-ric told her. "Emma, did you see old Ogden wield that sword! I didn't know he had it in him! He looked like a master swordsman!"

"They all did very well," I said. "But I think we should keep going. It looks as if Adara needs to sit down."

"I'm sorry if you didn't like it," Eadric told Adara. "But I really enjoy these reenactments. I think there may be another later tonight. Maybe we should try to catch that one, too. We don't have anything nearly this interesting at my parents' castle."

"Thank goodness!" said Adara. "Would you mind ter-ribly if we didn't stick around for any more? I think I've seen quite enough for one day."

"Whatever you want," Eadric said, sounding disap-pointed. "You're the guest."

We didn't have much farther to go before we reached my grandfather's rooms. "Here we are!" Eadric finally announced, and stopped to knock on a door.

The door swung open, revealing a room so dark that I couldn't see more than a few feet past the threshold. With a wave of my hand, I lit the candles my grandfather kept for visitors. The vague outline of King Aldrid floated above the floor, becoming more solid-looking as the candle flames grew.

"Grandfather!" I said, blowing him a kiss.

"Hello, my dear!" my grandfather replied in the hollow, breathy voice of a ghost. "It's so good to see you again. And Eadric! You're looking fit! Who is this you brought with you?"

"You're a ghost!" whispered Adara. "At first I thought they kept you down here because you were sick or insane, but you aren't even alive! Is this castle filled with ghosts?"

"Just the dungeon!" my grandfather said with a chuckle.

The princess moved so close to Eadric that he had to shift the torch he carried to his other hand so she didn't get burned.

"I've been a ghost for many years, as have most of my friends," said Grandfather. "Who are you again?"

"This is Princess Adara of Lower Mucksworthy," I told him. "She's descended from King Snodgrass and Queen Ermingarde."

"I knew Old Snoddy! He was quite sociable and loved to gamble. No one played dice with him more than once, though. The man was a terrible cheat."

"You knew my great-grandfather?" asked Adara.

"For a few years. He was old when I was young. He died two years after we met and didn't stick around as a ghost like I did. When I knew him, he was married to a woman named Phyllius. Very unpleasant woman, as I recall. I can't remember if she was his fourth or fifth wife. I don't remember any of his children, but I know he had a few," said the king. "Come in and sit down. Adara, I'd offer you refreshments, but I don't eat or drink. So, Emma, how is the kingdom faring?"

"Very well," I told him, "except two fairies came to see me."

"Fairies?" Adara said with a scornful laugh.

Grandfather glanced at Adara. "Never be disrespectful of fairies, young lady. They are very powerful and don't take kindly to ridicule of any sort." Turning back to me, he asked, "What did the fairies want? They don't generally come around unless it's something serious."

"It seems they're having problems in the enchanted forest," I told him. "Maple told me that the leaves on her trees are withering. Water Lily doesn't have enough water for her lilies. I did some research, but I couldn't find anything useful. Grassina told me that when she went to see Maple's trees, everything seemed normal, except for the leaves. I was wondering if you might have any ideas about how to deal with this."

"None at all," said Grandfather. "Although I agree that we should look into it. Simple problems are often the first signs of something much worse. Listen! What is that chattering sound?"

"My teeth," Adara declared. "It's really cold in here!"

"We should leave," I said, getting to my feet. "I should probably go to bed early tonight anyway. I have a lot to do tomorrow."

"Come back when you can," my grandfather said as we started for the door. "I get tired of talking to the same old ghosts telling the same old stories all the time. It's nice to see young people, who are still experiencing life!"

Adara was the first out the door. She waited for me to take the lead and insisted on walking next to Eadric. "You'll have to go behind me," he said.

"Why?" she asked. "The corridor is wide enough for two."

Eadric sighed. "Because you never know what you might run into down here. We need room to get out of the way."

"Out of the way of what?" Adara said. "There's nothing here. And even if there was, I'm sure you could protect me."

"If you want me to protect you, you need to walk behind me," said Eadric.

"I'll be fine right here," she said, keeping pace with him.

Eadric grunted, and I knew he wasn't happy.

We hadn't gone far before I had the unmistakable feeling that we were being watched. Although I tried to look everywhere at once, I didn't see anything. The feeling grew stronger until we had almost reached the stairs. Some of the torches had gone out, leaving part of the corridor in shadow. When I heard the scrape of claws on stone, I gestured for Eadric to raise the torch higher. Two red eyes reflected the light back at me.

"Look out!" I shouted as the shadow beast rushed us.

The shadow beast looked like a shadow the size of a week-old calf. What gave it away were its two glowing red eyes. Years ago, my aunt Grassina told me that the beast actually has substance and can hurt anyone who isn't careful. She taught me how to handle the beast, which seemed to be attracted to visitors in the dungeon. Remembering what Grassina taught me, I stood my ground until the very last second. The beast was almost on top of me when I stepped to the side and rapped it smartly between its eyes. Howling, the beast started to run deeper into the dungeon. Although Eadric jumped out of the way, Adara stood, looking around. With a shout, I grabbed her arm and yanked her to the side. She slammed into the wall and cried out in pain and surprise as the shadow beast ran past.

Adara turned and gave me a reproachful look. "Why did you do that?" she asked, rubbing her cheek.

"Because the shadow beast was about to run you down," I explained, and started walking again.

"I didn't see any shadow beast," grumbled Adara.

"It was there," Eadric said. "Believe me."

"Oh, I believe you, Eadric," Adara said, taking his arm.

"But not me, apparently," I muttered to myself.

We had reached the top of the stairs when Adara announced that she wasn't feeling well and was on her way to bed. She was walking away when a guard approached. He told me that someone was waiting to talk to me in the Great Hall. Eadric and I looked at each other, wondering who it could be at that hour. Following the guard, we entered the Hall and found a middle-aged man wearing the clothes of a farmer sitting on a bench by the door.

"I'm sorry to disturb you so late in the day, Your Highness, but I came right after I saw what had happened and it took me a while to get here," said the farmer. "I'm Johnson. My fields are next to the enchanted forest. I planted my crops there because of the fairies. They take good care of the forest, and the dust they use runs off into the fields around it, making them healthy, too. I've had some of my best harvests ever since I started planting those fields. I would have had a great harvest this year if this hadn't happened. It's my wheat, you see. Someone gave it the blight."

"I'm sorry to hear that, but I don't know what I can do about it," I told the man. "Haven't you ever dealt with the blight before?"

Johnson nodded. "Back before I planted near the forest, it happened every few years, but it was never like this. It's not the blight itself, you see. It's the way it hit my wheat. Some wheat has it and some doesn't. It's made a pattern like a big circle. Darndest thing I ever saw."

"Really?" I said. "You think someone might have infected your crop with the blight deliberately?"

"I can't think of any other reason it would look like that. Who would do such a thing to a man's wheat?"

"I don't know, but I'm going to find out," I replied. "I'll come look at it tomorrow."

First Maple and Water Lily, now Farmer Johnson. Something must be really wrong.

Five

adric had mentioned that he wanted to go to the enchanted forest with me, so I wasn't surprised when he brought Ferdy with him to breakfast. Ferdy was the singing sword Eadric had bought at the magic marketplace, and it was the best sword he had ever owned. I was hoping that we could leave Adara at the castle, and was happy to see that she hadn't come downstairs by the time we started our breakfast. Unfortunately, Eadric had to eat his usual three bowls of oatmeal and stack of buttered toast before we could go anywhere. By the time we started up the stairs to get my magic carpet, Adara had arrived.

I had already dragged my magic carpet out of the storage room and unrolled it on the floor, so it was ready when we climbed the tower stairs. The rug had been Grassina's, left behind when the curse took hold and she moved down to the dungeon. It was an older rug and had a few quirks, but the colors were still bright and I knew how to handle it. I'd also made a few modifications of my own.

I sat on one side and Eadric sat on the other. Adara, who had followed us upstairs, appeared baffled as she stood beside the rug. "What are you doing?" she asked. "I thought we were going to the enchanted forest this morning."

"We are," I said. "We'll see you when we get back."

"Why are you sitting on that ugly rug?" she asked.

I whispered a command and the carpet began to rise.

Adara gasped. "Is that a magic carpet? I've heard of them in stories, but I've never actually seen one before. Wait for me! I'm going, too!"

We were two feet off the ground when Adara tried to climb on between Eadric and me. There wasn't room for three people to ride side by side, so when I didn't move over, she jostled me and I fell off, tumbling to the floor.

"Why did you do that?" Eadric asked Adara. "That was really rude!" He got off to help me up, then laid a protective arm around my shoulders and glared at the princess.

The carpet kept rising because I hadn't done anything to stop it.

"Eadric?" asked Adara. "What are you doing? Don't you want to sit with me?"

"I want to sit with Emma," he replied, giving me an extra squeeze.

I glanced at the carpet. With only one person on it, the carpet was rising faster now. It was already at head height and would reach the high ceiling soon.

Adara squawked and peered over the edge. "What's happening?" she asked. "Is it supposed to do this?"

"Only if I'm not controlling it," I told her. "That's a safety feature so no one can steal it."

Adara looked up, then back down at me. "Isn't it going to stop?"

"Not unless I tell it to," I said. "It will go all the way to the ceiling and squash anyone who's on it."

The princess reached up to the ceiling that was getting closer by the second. Placing both hands against it, she tried to keep the rug from going higher. "Make it stop!" she shouted. "What are you waiting for?"

"I'm waiting for you to promise that you won't do that kind of thing again. You took my seat last night and again today. There's a reason I sit where I do. I'm the Green Witch. This is my home and my rug. You are a guest, so I've made allowances for you, but you cannot take my place. Ask me nicely and you can go with us, but you'll have to do what I say and be more respectful."

The carpet was already only a little over a foot from the ceiling. Adara had lain down on her stomach and was peering over the edge at me again. "I promise!" she shouted "Now get me down from here!"

"Say *please*," I told her.

"Please!" she cried as her back touched the ceiling.

I gestured and the carpet stopped moving.

"Would it really have squashed her?" Eadric whispered in my ear.

"No," I whispered back. "But it would have held her against the ceiling until I let her down."

I gestured again and the carpet began to descend. In a few seconds, it was hovering beside me at waist height. While Adara scooted farther back on the carpet, Eadric and I climbed on. "Eadric, why don't you sit back here with me?" she asked him.

"Because he's sitting up here with me like he always does," I said through gritted teeth. "No talking now, please. I have to concentrate while I'm doing this."

Eadric snorted. He knew that I could make the carpet fly while I was half-asleep. Because he didn't say anything, I was sure he didn't want to listen to Adara's chatter any more than I did.

I made the carpet rise another foot, then race toward the window. The opening was much narrower than the carpet, so it looked as if we'd never fit, but at the last second the window widened like a big smile, letting us pass through unscathed. When I glanced back, Adara was gripping the sides of the carpet, her face white and her lips pressed into a thin line. "Oh, I forgot," I said. A few muttered words and the ropes that held the passengers in place whipped around our waists, tightening themselves so we couldn't fall off.

We were halfway to the enchanted forest when I took out my farseeing ball. "Show me the route to Farmer Johnson's crops beside the enchanted forest," I said. I began scanning the ground as we drew closer, thinking that the blight-stricken plants might be hard to see, but I needn't have bothered. Even from a distance, the afflicted plants stood out. Farmer Johnson was right: the blight had affected plants in a very specific pattern, but it wasn't just one circle; it was three concentric circles with the shape of a flower in the middle. The withered plants were brown, compared to the vivid green plants around them, making quite a contrast.

"I think it's kind of pretty," I said, pointing it out to Eadric.

"Huh," he said. "Why would anyone do that?"

"Do you see anything that might have caused it?" I asked as we went lower.

"Not from here. Why don't you set the carpet down so we can look around?"

"Can you put us on the ground really fast?" asked Adara. "I think I'm about to be sick."

"Right away!" I replied, worried about my carpet.

The moment we landed, Adara hurried off by herself while Eadric and I looked around. We didn't see anything, including footprints, and were soon climbing back onto the carpet. We had to wait a few minutes for Adara to return. When she did, she looked slightly green. Once we were all

50

settled, I took out my farseeing ball again. "Where is Water Lily's pond?" I asked it.

The enchanted forest was so large that it covered much of northern Greater Greensward. It varied from stands of ancient trees deep with shadows and secrets to sun-filled glades where unicorns cropped sweetgrass and fairies played among wildflowers. With creatures both nasty and benign dwelling in the forest, it was an uncertain place to venture.

Following the route the farseeing ball showed me, we entered the forest, flying just above the ground. We hadn't gone far when we heard the sound of large wings beating the air and snapping twigs behind us. When I looked back, a half-grown griffin was following us through the trees. While the adult griffins that lived in the enchanted forest knew enough to leave me alone, the younger ones had yet to learn just how dangerous I could be.

I made the carpet go faster, hoping to outrun the griffin. Its eagle eyes lit up and its eagle wings beat that much harder. The griffin seemed to think it was a game, following us turn for turn. Finally, we were in danger of passing the very spot I wanted to inspect, so I turned around and flicked my fingers at it. Sparks shot from my fingertips, streaming past Adara, who screamed and would have fallen off if not for the rope wrapped around her waist.

Although the griffin tried to avoid the sparks, they followed it, exploding in sparkling puffs inches from its eagle beak. The beast let out a high-pitched scream as it turned and fled, its lion tail between its legs.

"That was fun!" Eadric declared, grinning.

"It was, wasn't it?" I said, grinning back at him.

"That was terrifying!" exclaimed Adara. "What is wrong with you people?"

"You should have stayed back at the castle," Eadric said over his shoulder. "Any trip into the enchanted forest is dangerous."

When we landed beside Water Lily's pond, I saw what the fairy had meant. The water was much lower than it should have been, with the level only halfway to the high-water mark. Usually the water lilies' stems were submerged, but now they lay across the surface of the water, twining around one another to form a triangle with a cluster of small leaves in the middle.

"Look, another pattern," I told Eadric. "Who do you suppose is making them?"

Eadric scratched his head. "This must mean something to somebody."

"Let's go see Maple's trees," I said.

We climbed back on the carpet and were soon in the air again. Adara sat with her lips pursed, not talking to either of us. She perked up when we passed a herd of unicorns running through an open field. I glanced at the farseeing ball and saw the route we needed to take to reach Maple's trees. We'd have to go through one of the older, darker parts of the forest. It was the very same place where we had first met the baby dragon Ralf when Eadric freed him from a giant web.

Eadric recognized the area after we'd gone only a little way. "Watch out for webs, Emma," he said, taking Ferdy from the sheath.

I slowed the carpet, trying to see through the gloom. "I can't see a thing," I finally told Eadric. "For all I know there might be hundreds of webs around us. Maybe we should go higher so we're above the trees."

"What are you talking about?" asked Adara. "Are you afraid of a little spider?"

"Not a little one," I said.

I stopped the carpet right where it was and held out my hands. With a few muttered words, I created a witch's light and sent it to hover over the ground a few yards in front of us. It was enough to let us see what lay before us as well as a few yards to each side. I started to look for a gap between the trees so we could fly above them, but they were growing too close to each other. Soft rustlings made me turn my head quickly. A short, staccato clicking made Eadric brandish Ferdy, which sang:

> Spiders fast and spiders slow,
> You're no match for me.
> I'll slice off your hairy legs and—

"Shh!" I told the sword. "We don't want to attract their attention if we can help it!"

"Got it!" the sword replied, and began to hum softly.

"You've got a singing sword, Eadric?" Adara asked in a normal voice.

"Shh!" Eadric told her, giving her a sharp look.

"There! I see one!" I cried, spotting the shine of the witch's light reflecting off the silvery web. "And there's another over there!"

Eadric pointed Ferdy in the direction of the webs. A spider as big as a small horse skittered across the closest web, making that same staccato clicking that we had heard only moments before. There was a rustling among the leaves on the forest floor, and an even bigger spider lunged at the carpet. Eadric slashed at the spider, knocking it to the ground.

When the spider started after us again, I said, "Oh, forget this!" and made the carpet zig and zag, rising until we were above the tops of the trees.

"I was about to kill that spider!" Eadric exclaimed.

"I know," I said. "But that's not why we're here today. We can come back another day and take care of all of them."

"Eadric, you are so brave!" Adara cried. "I would have gladly watched you slay each and every spider, if only Emma wasn't afraid of them."

"Oh, please!" I said as I turned the carpet around.

It wasn't as easy to follow directions given for ground travel when we were flying higher, but it didn't take us much longer to find the maple trees. From the air, the trees with the dried, withered leaves stood out among their healthy neighbors, and it was easy to see that there was a pattern, just like there had been with the wheat and the water lilies. This pattern was diamond shaped, with the curve of a leaf in the middle.

Landing the carpet, Eadric and I got off to look around. The fairy Maple wasn't there, and neither was anyone else. It was unusually quiet except for the crunch of dead leaves beneath our feet. Other than brown leaves hanging from the trees when they should have been supple and green, we didn't see anything unusual.

"I don't know what's causing this, but one thing is obvious," I told Eadric. "It isn't natural. Someone has to be behind this. But I can't imagine who it might be."

Six

"Maybe the patterns mean something," said Adara.

"I'm sure they do, but I've never seen them before," Eadric replied

"I haven't, either," I told him. "I guess we should make copies of the patterns and show them around."

"I'll do it!" said Eadric. "I'm good at drawing. Anyone have parchment, a quill, and a pot of ink handy?"

Two bright lights fluttered down from the sky, landing at the edge of the trees. "I'm so mad, I could spit!" one of the fairies said as she became full-sized. It was Maple and she was talking to Aspen, a fairy I'd seen before. "Why would she do that to my trees? What have I ever done to her?"

"She said she didn't do it," said Aspen. "I've never known her to lie."

"Of course she did it!" Maple exclaimed. "Who else would make that mark? You said yourself that it's the symbol of her campaign!"

"Excuse me," I said, crunching dead leaves as I walked toward the fairies. "Did you find out who did this to your trees?"

"You came!" said Maple. "Good! Maybe you can do something about her. It was Sumac, I'm sure of it. That's the symbol of her campaign right there for all to see." She pointed at the sad-looking trees and shivered when another leaf fell. "I didn't see the whole thing until I looked at it from the air. Aspen pointed out that it was Sumac's campaign symbol."

"What campaign?" I asked, confused.

"For the new Fairy Queen," Aspen explained. "Sumac is running against Chervil and Poppy."

"Does one of them have a symbol that's a triangle with little leaves in the middle?" asked Eadric.

"Or three circles with a flower in the center?" I said.

"Why, yes," said Maple. "Poppy's is the one with the flower, and Chervil's is the triangle with the little leaves. Why do you ask?"

"Because we've found those symbols written in other plants," I told them. "Water Lily and a farmer came to see me after you did, Maple. Their plants were damaged, too."

"Why is anyone running for Fairy Queen? What happened to the one you have?" asked Eadric.

"She's gone," said Aspen. "We think she faded away."

"You mean she died?" asked Adara.

"Fairies don't really die," Maple told her. "I thought

everyone knew that. When we've lived so long that nothing seems exciting or interesting anymore, we just fade away. It doesn't happen very often, but it does happen."

"We all miss Queen Willow," said Aspen. "She was a lovely person, a good and just queen, and a very powerful fairy, but lately she's kept to herself. No one has seen her in oh so long. The real problem is that she never chose anyone to succeed her."

"Willow was the queen? Isn't she the fairy who gave the ring and title to the first Green Witch?" asked Eadric. "Remember, Emma? That old fairy was wearing willow leaves."

I nodded. Eadric and I had met her at the first Green Witch's birthday party when we went back in time. "I remember her. My whole family is indebted to your queen for giving us such a wonderful gift. I'm so sorry to hear that she's faded away."

"Me too," said Maple. "Now the fairies are trying to decide who will be queen next."

"Or king," said Aspen. "Although we haven't had one of those in a very long time."

"Chervil, Poppy, and Sumac are the only ones who came forward," said Maple. "Now we have to decide which one we want to rule us fairies. The problem is, I don't like any of them. I never have and I never will."

"You're just mad that someone hurt your trees," said Aspen.

"I'm not the only one who doesn't like them," Maple told her. "I heard that fairies were fighting over who would be the least awful candidate. Besides, the one who hurt my trees had to be Sumac. Who else would use her symbol?"

"But I told you, she said she didn't and I believe her," replied Aspen.

"This is where we came in on this conversation," said Eadric.

"Where can I find Sumac now?" I asked.

"Last I heard, she was campaigning at the edge of the enchanted forest," said Aspen. "You know, over by the swamp near your castle."

"Then that's where we'll head next," I told Eadric. "Get back on the carpet, Adara. We're going to go meet the possible future Fairy Queen."

❧

I knew the swamp well, having spent much of my time there when I was younger. It was where I had gone to get away from my mother. It was also where Eadric and I had met and fallen in love. When I was young, the part of the swamp that bordered the enchanted forest had been my least favorite and I usually avoided going there. My aunt Grassina had warned me that bears, wolves, and the occasional dragon visited the pond at the very edge, so I knew just how unsafe it could be. I hadn't been there in ages, so I was interested in seeing if it had changed.

Taking the most direct route out of the forest, we followed the border until we reached the swamp. It looked much the same, with meandering streams crisscrossing the soggy ground and small hillocks offering the only real footing. I was showing them some pretty purple flowers when Adara said, "That's odd!" and pointed at the ground. "Someone has been walking around in bare feet."

Eadric peered over the edge and shook his head. "An ordinary person didn't make those tracks. Follow the footprints back a few yards and you'll see that they started out as paw prints. That was a werewolf."

"A werewolf!" Adara cried with a shudder. "Are we safe here? Maybe we should go higher so it can't jump onto the carpet and bite us!"

"We're safe," Eadric said, patting his sword. "No werewolf can stand up to Ferdy. Say, is that a blackberry patch? Even from up here those berries look really good!"

Eadric leaned so far toward the edge that he would have fallen off if not for the strap holding him on. His weight made the carpet sag on that side and we were in danger of tipping over. "Be careful," I said, grabbing his shoulder and pulling him back.

"Do you mind if we stop here for a few minutes?" he asked. "I'm hungry again."

"After we do what we came here for," I said. I had just caught a glimpse of movement and bright colors and had a feeling I'd found the fairies.

"I would let you if it were up to me, Eadric," said Adara.

"Business first," I said, turning the carpet. "Do you see that group of people over there?"

Eadric nodded. "Fairies, if I'm not mistaken. The colorful hair always gives them away. It sounds as if they're arguing."

"Maple and Aspen did say that fairies were fighting over the candidates," I reminded him.

"Yes, but it looks like they're fighting with the candidates, too," he replied. "That's probably Sumac on the stump."

"Stop carrying on and listen to me!" shouted the fairy girl with dark red hair who was standing on an old tree stump. "I know what I'm talking about. I'm smart and talented and can solve all our problems. The first thing we're going to do is cut all ties with humans!"

A chorus of protest broke out. Finally one voice shouted above the rest, "Why would we want to do that?"

"Don't you understand? Humans should all be banned from the forest!" Sumac shouted as we drew closer. "Humans cut down trees and hunt our friends the forest creatures. They pillage our plants, stealing the berries, flowers, and herbs we work so hard to grow."

"How do you suggest we keep them out, exactly?" shouted a fairy with long pink hair.

"I know just what to do!" Sumac cried. "No one is

better at planning ahead than me. We'll put up a magical wall around the forest to keep humans out. Keep the forest for the fairies!"

"Your magic isn't strong enough to put up a wall like that," hollered a fairy from the rear of the crowd.

"It will be after I get Willow's magic wand!" Sumac shouted back. "Then I'll be as strong as she ever was!"

Some of the fairies grumbled and others laughed. Only a few seemed to take Sumac seriously. The ones who disagreed with her were the loudest, however. "Not all humans are bad!" called out a stocky fairy in a coat of bark. "Some of my best friends are human!"

"Mine, too!" another fairy added.

A few members of the audience stomped off, angry. I set the carpet on the ground only yards from Sumac and got to my feet. When it looked as if her meeting might be breaking up, I waved to get her attention.

"What do you want, human?" Sumac asked in a rude voice.

A number of fairies heard her and came back to listen.

"I'm here on behalf of the fairy Maple. She asks why you put your design on her trees and wants you to stop it. Needless to say, she's very upset."

Sumac spluttered and glanced at the fairies who had gathered closer. "What are you talking about?" she asked me. "I didn't do anything to her trees!"

"Maple is sure you did it. Someone defaced her trees with the design that you use as your symbol. Why would anyone but you do that?"

Sumac turned to face the other fairies. "Do you see why we need to ban them from our forest? Interfering busybodies! What makes you think you have a right to get involved in fairy business, anyway?" she said, turning back to me.

I noticed that the looks some of the fairies were giving me weren't very friendly.

"I'm the Green Witch," I told them. "Years ago your queen gave members of my family the title and the responsibility of watching out for the humans and fairies in Greater Greensward. Maple came to me about her trees and I promised to look into it."

The fairies nodded when I mentioned the old queen and began whispering to one another, turning their unfriendly looks on Sumac.

"It wasn't me!" said Sumac. "I already told Aspen that."

"Do I know you?" asked a fairy. I glanced her way and saw that it was the Swamp Fairy and she was studying me closely. "You look awfully familiar."

The last time Eadric and I had encountered the Swamp Fairy, he had insulted her. She had been about to cast a spell on him when Olefat interrupted. I was still grateful for the help he'd given us.

Turning aside, I whispered to Eadric, "Why don't you take Adara back to that berry patch. We might be a while." The patch was far enough away that the Swamp Fairy wouldn't be able to see him. We would have a real problem if she remembered how rude he had been to her.

"Sounds like a good idea," he said, his eyes lighting up. "Holler if you need me."

"Maybe a human made that pattern," said Sumac. "They're always hurting our plants!"

I shook my head. "It couldn't have been a human. You can't see the pattern unless you're flying overhead."

"No human could hurt those trees if we put up that wall!" Sumac said, looking at the other fairies again.

"I know I've seen you somewhere recently," said the Swamp Fairy. "If only I can remember where."

"How are you going to keep some people out and let others in?" I asked Sumac. "Will you allow wolves into your forest?"

"Of course!" said Sumac. "All forest creatures will still be welcome there."

"What about werewolves?" I asked. "They're human part of the time. And there are other creatures that can turn into humans when they want to. Are you going to ban all of them, too?"

"It's right on the tip of my brain," said the Swamp Fairy.

Sumac gave me a scornful look. "Fairies can tell when someone isn't fully human."

"Is that so?" I asked. "Then what am I, exactly?"

"You're a human, of course," said Sumac. "Anyone can tell that."

"I'm human right now, but I'm not always," I told her.

I had already begun to change when the Swamp Fairy gave a triumphant shout. "I remember now! You were with that boy who insulted me just the other day! I was about to turn you both into mushrooms, but you ran away too fast."

I had been practicing the change and was getting quite good at the transformation, although the sheer excitement still took my breath away. Time seemed to stand still, at least for me, as I turned into a dragon. Everyone watching froze, although I didn't know if it was from fear or surprise. The Swamp Fairy stopped moving, with her hand raised to point at me. Sumac paused in a mid-shake of denial. Then there I was, a pale green dragon with fire already burning in my belly.

I stretched my neck so that my face was only inches from Sumac's and said, "It seems to me that you're not that good at telling who is human and who might be something else."

In an instant, most of the fairies turned tiny and fled. Only Sumac, frozen under my gaze, remained behind. "I didn't know!" she said. "Please don't eat me or burn me to a crisp!"

"I wouldn't dream of it," I told her, and sat back on my

65

haunches. "Now that we're alone, are you sure you weren't the one to damage Maple's trees?"

"It wasn't me, I swear!" cried Sumac. "It was probably one of my rivals. Go talk to Chervil and Poppy. I bet one of them did it."

"And where would I find them?" I asked.

"The last I heard, Poppy was visiting the fairies who live near the Old Witches' Retirement Community. The witches are letting her use their commons for a rally."

"And what about Chervil?" I asked.

Whoomp! Whoomp! The sound of enormous wings drowned out whatever Sumac might have been about to say. In a flash, she turned tiny and fled into the forest, leaving me to face the two dragons landing near me. Although I recognized them, it was obvious from the look on Grumble Belly's face that he didn't recognize me. The huge, blue-black dragon was intimidating even when he was being friendly. Suspicious and wary, the adult male dragon was terrifying. Huddled beside him, his little son, Ralf, just looked puzzled.

"Who are you and what are you doing here?" Grumble Belly demanded, his hot breath washing over me.

"It's me, Emma!" I exclaimed. I had turned into a dragon the first time in order to stop a magical fight between my aunt and my grandmother, both of whom were under the influence of the family curse. I hadn't seen my dragon friends since then, so neither one would know that I could turn into a dragon, something most witches would find impossible.

"Emma who?" asked Grumble Belly.

"I'm the one who became a Dragon Friend when I helped Ralf at the Dragon Olympics!" I told them. "Hi, Ralf! It's good to see you again."

"Papa, is that really Emma?" whispered Ralf. "She's green! I've never seen a dragon her color before."

"Look, I'll prove it!" I cried. A moment later, I stood before them as the human they remembered.

"It is you!" Ralf shouted. "You can turn into a dragon now! I thought you could only turn into a frog! Wow! This is great! Now we can do all sorts of things together. Can Eadric turn into a dragon, too?"

I laughed and shook my head. "No, just me. I think I can do it only because I'm a Dragon Friend. As far as I know, I'm the only human who can turn into a dragon."

"Hey, Ralf! Hi, Grumble Belly!" Eadric shouted, hurrying to join us. "What are you doing here?"

"We were flying home when we saw Emma," said Ralf.

"And now that we've spoken with her, we need to go," said his father. "I promised I would catch tonight's supper."

Ralf smiled. "Mama is helping me learn flaming. Papa is giving me flying lessons. Someday I'll be as good at flaming as Mama and fly as fast as Papa. Right?" he said, looking up at his father.

"That's right, son," the huge dragon said, gazing fondly

at Ralf before turning back to me. "I know his mother and I said he was too young to start flaming, but he really wanted to and he's been very well-behaved lately. He's been practicing a lot over the last few weeks."

Ralf nodded. "I started eating gunga beans and flami-peppers after the Dragon Olympics last month. You should see how long I can make my flame! My flying is getting better, too. Papa says that someday I'll be faster than he is!"

"I bet you will," I said with a smile. The Dragon Olympics were a yearly event. Ralf had taken Eadric and me to the games the year before. Ralf was too young to compete, but his mother had won the contest for the longest flame.

"Come along, son. We really have to go," said his father.

"We'll see you soon, Emma and Eadric!" Ralf shouted as he took to the air.

I watched until they disappeared above the trees of the enchanted forest. When I turned to say something to Eadric, Adara started talking first. "I can't believe you had a conversation with two dragons! You have a sword with you, Eadric. Why didn't you slay them both? The little one would have been easy to kill!"

Horrified, Eadric and I turned to glare at her. "Those dragons are friends of ours," said Eadric. "I would never hurt either of them!"

"You can't make friends with dragons!" Adara declared. "They aren't people, they're lizards. No animal is the equal

of a human! Trying to be friends with them isn't natural!"
Turning on her heel, she flounced toward the carpet.

"They may be lizards, but they're nicer than a lot of people we know!" I said. When Eadric and I took our seats on the carpet, I might have made it start flying again a little faster than necessary, and I might have made Adara flop backward on purpose, but there was only so much that I could put up with from anyone!

Seven

The Old Witches' Retirement Community was located farther north in the enchanted forest. Home to many of the older witches who lived in Greater Greensward, it was a comfortable place and always well-maintained through spells and other witchy contributions. Because my grandmother Olivene had long made it her home, I had visited it often.

Unlike the swamp, the Old Witches' Retirement Community had changed a lot since my childhood days. Many of the witches had moved on, either because they'd died or because they'd found someplace else they'd rather live. Nearly a dozen witches had chosen to stay on the island that Olefat the wizard had tricked them into visiting. An overweight witch had used a spell to make herself lighter and had floated off into the clouds. It was rumored that she was currently living on the moon. Two witches had turned themselves into foxes, then forgotten how to turn themselves back. They lived deeper in the forest now, visiting the Community only on special occasions.

With so many witches gone, their unoccupied cottages had either walked away on chicken legs, been eaten by passing children, or crumbled into dust when their spells weren't renewed. Once the vacancies were announced, other witches had moved in, selecting more modern cottages that were larger and more spacious inside. Even the older cottages that remained didn't look quite the same. My grandmother had replaced many of her chewed gingerbread walls with a new recipe that tasted sweeter and was a darker shade of brown. The spun sugar she used to decorate the eaves looked more delicate, and the gumdrops more sugary.

"I like what your grandmother has done with the place!" Eadric said as we landed in her front yard. Since our last visit, she had installed a gate made of fruit-flavored lozenges and replaced the window shutters with sugar wafers.

"You'll have to tell Grandmother that," I said as I got off the carpet.

"I will, as soon as I've tasted everything!" he said, licking his lips.

"Someone actually lives here?" Adara said as she got off the carpet. "You'd have to be crazy to live in a house like this!"

"That was rude!" said a big orange-striped cat as he

strolled out of the flower bed. "Too bad she's not a bird or a mouse. I'd teach her a thing or two. Maybe I will anyway." Lifting a paw, he unsheathed his claws and glanced at Adara.

"Leave her alone, Herald," I told the cat. "She's with us."

"All the more reason to introduce her to these," he said, and licked his claws.

"Who are you talking to?" Adara asked me as she looked around. "There's no one here except us and that scruffy-looking cat."

"Why, I oughta—" Herald began.

"Do nothing," I told him. "She can't understand you, so she thinks you don't have feelings." The only humans who could understand animals were the ones who'd once been turned into animals themselves. Even Eadric, who had once been a frog, could talk to the animals he met.

The door opened and my grandmother stepped out. "I thought I heard your voice, Emma! I'm so glad you and Eadric stopped by. Oh, you brought *her* with you," she said, frowning at Adara. "I thought she'd have gone home by now."

"We're looking for the fairy named Poppy," I told my grandmother. "I was told she was holding a rally here, but I didn't see her when we flew over the Community."

"She is, or at least she will be. It should be starting in an hour or so. Just a moment and I'll see what time it is now." Grandmother stepped out of her cottage, closing her door behind her. It was only a few steps to a new sundial with a chocolate-chip-cookie face.

"What happened to your old sundial?" Eadric asked.

"Someone ate it while I was away. I like this one better anyway. The big chocolate chip tells the time much more precisely. Look, it's just as I said. We have a whole hour before the rally starts. Why don't we have a picnic lunch while we're waiting?"

"Sounds good to me!" said Eadric.

While Grandmother brought out the food, Eadric and I spread a blanket on the ground. "What's that for?" asked Adara.

"We're going to sit on it to eat our lunch," said Eadric. "Haven't you ever had a picnic lunch before?"

"I've never sat on the ground before," Adara declared, casting a scornful look at the blanket.

"That's because Princess Adara is from Lower Mucksworthy," Grandmother said as she came out the door carrying a tray. "The ground there is never dry enough to sit on. Most of her kingdom is covered in mud."

Eadric hurried to take the tray from my grandmother. "Then you should really enjoy this!" he told Adara.

Adara gave him a brilliant smile. "I'm sure I will!" she told him, but I noticed that she made a disgusted face when she glanced at the blanket again.

"Why don't you sit over there," Grandmother said to Adara, pointing to a spot on the blanket.

When Adara saw that she would be sitting next to Eadric, she gathered her skirts under her and sat where my grandmother had suggested. I glanced at Grandmother, wondering if she was up to something. Although the curse had made her a horrible person, she had become kind and sweet once the curse was over. Unfortunately, the way she had been acting toward Adara reminded me more of her old, awful self.

Eadric helped himself to dried fish, bread, cheese, and nearly half the fruit tarts, while grandmother handed around mugs of juice. When the rest of us helped ourselves, I noticed that Adara took very little and only picked at her food. I was about to suggest that she try one of the tarts before Eadric ate them all when I noticed that Herald was flattened to the ground, tail twitching, a few yards behind her.

Adara took a sip of her juice and made a face. She was setting her mug back on the blanket when she suddenly yelped and started slapping at her legs.

"Is something wrong, dear?" Grandmother asked, sounding a little too innocent.

"There are ants all over my legs!" Adara cried. "They're biting me!"

Herald wiggled his back end and launched himself at Adara. When he landed on her with his claws out, the princess shrieked, jumped to her feet, and knocked over her mug of juice.

Herald ran off with his tail straight up, looking pleased with himself.

"Really, Herald! I don't know what's gotten into you!" Grandmother cried.

"Are you all right?" I asked Adara.

"Just fine!" she replied through gritted teeth.

"Would you like more juice?" I asked her, holding up the pitcher.

"No thanks!" she said. "The first mug was too sour."

I glanced at Grandmother, who just smiled and shrugged. I decided that it was time to leave.

When I turned to look toward the center of the Community, a cloud of twinkling lights was already descending on the area around the big fire pit. "Look!" I said. "The fairies who want to hear Poppy are starting to arrive."

The cottages were built around a large, open area where the witches held ceremonies, rituals, and weekly potluck suppers. Tables and benches surrounded the fire pit that sat at the very center. Even now, in the middle of the day, the fire in the pit was burning.

"Do you want to head over there now?" I asked my friends. "We should be able to get good seats if we hurry."

"We might as well," Adara said, brushing the last of the ants off her gown.

"Do you know Poppy?" I asked Grandmother as we started toward the pit.

"We all do," she replied. "She's very popular in the Community. Her flowers brighten nearly everyone's gardens. She's here all the time anyway, so it made sense that she'd hold her rally in the commons. Ah, there she is now."

Where Sumac's hair was a dark, muted shade of red, Poppy's was a brilliant orange-red that would be prominent in any crowd. She was standing by the fire pit, waving to the new arrivals as each one grew from a tiny fairy into human-sized. When everyone was there, she climbed onto a table and turned to face her audience.

"I've come to talk to you today about the path I think fairy-kind should take in the future. After years of observing humans closely, I believe that it's time for us to be more than observers. It's time for fairies to step in and help our friends the humans."

"Why do you think we should do that?" called a fairy.

"Because she's a tender-hearted nitwit!" cried one of the witches who had gathered to watch.

"Because we have magic and most of them don't!" shouted Poppy. "Aside from our witch and wizard friends, humans don't have magic to tie their own shoes without bending over, let alone solve important problems like chasing away harpies. You have to feel sorry for them, toiling away their whole lives just to keep their children safe and put food on their tables!"

"And putting up with goody-goodies like you telling them how lousy they have it!" shouted another witch.

"What do you have in mind?" called my grandmother.

"We'll help humans when they need it," said Poppy.

"And what do we get out of it?" called a fairy with purple hair in the front row.

"I suppose they'll have to give us something in return," said Poppy. "Like bowls of fresh cream to drink and warm places to stay in the winter."

"You make us sound like cats!" yelled another fairy. "I'm not helping anyone for cream or a dusty corner."

"What kind of help would you give the humans?" shouted the witch next to her. "Can *you* chase away harpies?"

"If I had Willow's wand, I could," said Poppy.

"Can you make the sun shine on a cloudy day like Queen Willow could?" called another witch.

"Maybe, if I had her wand," Poppy told her.

A fairy in the middle of the group raised her hand. "How are you going to talk all the fairies into helping all the humans?"

Poppy shrugged. "I haven't worked that part out yet."

"This plan is more half-baked than my last birthday cake!" cried a white-haired witch.

Whispering among themselves, the fairies began to leave. The witches were even less polite.

"Well, that was a waste of time!" one witch declared in a loud voice.

"I wasn't expecting to hear such a ridiculous scheme!" announced another as she stomped off. "My pet weasel could have come up with something better than that!"

"I thought the witches liked Poppy," Adara said to my grandmother.

"They do," she replied. "You should hear what they say when they don't like someone. It's enough to curl your ear hairs!"

Wanting to talk to Poppy before she flew off, I hurried to the table where the fairy still stood, looking dejected.

"Now what?" she asked as I drew closer. "Did you come to point out more flaws in my plan?"

I shook my head. "Actually, I came to see you about something else entirely. Do you know anything about the plants that were damaged to create the candidates' symbols? Whoever did it used a blight to draw your symbol in Farmer Johnson's wheat. The leaves on some of Maple's trees are withered to show Sumac's symbol, and Water Lily's pond was partly drained so that the lilies made the symbol belonging to Chervil. You can see the symbols best from the air."

"I don't know what you're talking about," Poppy said, looking puzzled. "Why would anyone damage plants to draw pictures?"

"That's what I'm wondering," I replied.

"So you're saying that you didn't do it?" Eadric asked as he joined us.

"Of course I didn't do it!" Poppy said, starting to look angry. "What a horrible accusation!"

"Do you think Chervil might have, then?" Eadric continued.

"I don't know anyone who would do such a terrible thing!" cried Poppy. "No decent fairy would even consider it."

"Uh-huh," Eadric said, rubbing his chin.

"Do you know where we might be able to find Chervil?" I asked Poppy.

"I think he's meeting some fairies in the garden of two witches. Ocu-something or other is the name of one of them," said Poppy.

"Oculura and Dyspepsia!" I cried. "I know them well. Then that's where we're going next."

"Do you mind if I go with you?" asked Poppy. "I'd like to see who showed up to listen to Chervil. A lot of fairies who had promised to come to my rally weren't here. I want to know if they've already gone over to his side."

"I don't mind at all," I told her.

We were heading toward my carpet when Adara caught up with me. "Why are you spending so much time looking for someone who damaged some leaves?"

"Because I promised I would," I replied. Even more, I was curious about who might end up replacing a Fairy Queen I hadn't really known but who had already proven to be better suited for the job than the candidates I'd met so far. I was beginning to worry that we might be headed for more trouble than we realized.

Eight

"*Y*ou can't ride with us!" Adara announced when she saw Poppy eyeing the carpet. "There isn't room!"

"I don't need a ride," the fairy replied. "It's just that I've never seen a magic carpet up close before. How does it work?"

"I tell it what to do," I said. "It listens to people with the right kind of magic. Do you know the way to Oculura and Dyspepsia's cottage?"

The fairy shook her head. "I've heard about it, but I've never been there."

"Then follow us," I told her. "It's easier to show the way than it is to give directions."

As soon as the carpet started rising, Poppy became tiny and darted over to me. She flew beside me the entire way, a silent companion I didn't mind at all.

❧

I had mixed feelings about visiting the witches Oculura and Dyspepsia. Although I had become friends with the sisters, the memories of my first visit to their home still made me uneasy. The cottage had once belonged to Vannabe, a woman without any magical abilities who thought she could learn to be a witch by reading a real witch's books. Searching for ingredients for a spell, she had captured Eadric and me. We were frogs at the time, and unable to help ourselves until I read a spell from a different book. In the meantime, we had to spend a very unpleasant night in the cottage, afraid that we were about to die.

I still couldn't return to the cottage without my stomach churning. Eadric didn't seem to mind it nearly as much. He looked around with interest as I landed the carpet.

"They fixed it up!" he said. "That roof is new and the cottage has more windows now."

"What a lovely garden!" Adara cried as Poppy darted off. "Would you like to explore it with me?"

"I can't right now," I told her.

"I was asking Eadric," she announced, turning to smile at him.

Eadric glanced at the cottage. "Maybe in a few minutes. I want to see inside." He hurried off without sparing her another look.

Adara sighed. "Queen Frazzela warned me that this might be difficult, but I never thought it would be this hard!" she said under her breath.

I turned to her, startled, but she was already wandering off into the garden. Were Adara and Eadric's mother plotting something? Precisely what was the difficult thing Adara was trying to do? Worried, I looked around for Eadric. When I saw that he was already halfway to the cottage, I hurried to catch up.

The witches had put a lot of work into the area near the cottage. A large garden in full bloom surrounded the little building, filling the air with a heady fragrance. Flowering fruit trees marked the garden's corners. I saw at least two fountains and three birdbaths, and that was just in front of the cottage. The brilliant blooms weren't the only source of color, however. Full-sized fairies dressed in brilliant hues walked between the rows while their tiny friends fluttered from one blossom to another, tasting nectar and exclaiming over the vivid display.

"It looks more like a party than a rally," Eadric said when I joined him. "Is that Oculura carrying a platter?"

Eadric and I had met Oculura at the magic marketplace while looking for an ingredient for the spell to turn Haywood from an otter to a man. Although Oculura had later introduced me to her sister, Dyspepsia, Eadric had never met her.

"They're serving food!" Eadric exclaimed, quickening his pace. "I wonder what it is."

While Eadric hurried toward Oculura, I looked around, hoping to spot Chervil. Unfortunately, I had no idea what the fairy looked like. "Is Chervil here?" I asked a passing fairy.

"He's in the garden behind the cottage," the fairy replied. "He said he'll start his speech soon. Have you tried the puff pastries? They're delicious!"

When I rejoined Eadric, Adara had found him again and had her hand on his arm. "I'm going to get some," she declared. "I didn't eat much at lunch. Eadric, are the pastries any good?"

Eadric was about to pop another pastry into his mouth, but he paused long enough to say, "They're wonderful!"

"Emma!" Oculura called from only a few yards away. "Is that you? I really can't tell. I put two new eyes in this morning. They're from a pair of cousins who never could see eye to eye. Everything is a little blurry. They've been giving me a headache, but I haven't had time to change them. Come inside with me while I get more pastries. I can change my eyes and we can talk. We can't be long, though. Chervil is going to start his speech soon and I don't want to miss a word!"

I followed her inside, with Eadric and Adara trailing behind us. The cottage looked very different from the first time I saw it. The room was cleaner now and the sisters had replaced most of the furniture, including the bed and table that Vannabe had used. The only thing hanging from the new ceiling was a lantern made of brass. I was relieved that the changes made it seem like a different room.

"Can I take some of these?" Eadric asked, pointing at the pastries cooling on the table.

"Help yourself!" Oculura told him. "I made plenty!"

After helping himself to a handful, Eadric wandered out the door, munching.

"Do you know Chervil very well?" I asked Oculura.

"Oh, my, yes!" she replied. "I've grown his plants in my gardens no matter where I've lived. We've known each other since I was just a girl. That's why I said he could have his rally here. He's such a dear and gets along with everyone. Even Dyspepsia likes him, and she hardly likes anyone. Ah, here we are!" Oculura took the jar of eyeballs from the shelf and shook it. The jar seemed fuller than it had the last time I was there.

"Are those real?" asked Adara.

I gave her an annoyed glance before turning back to Oculura. "This is Princess Adara from Lower Mucksworthy. She wanted to come with us today."

"How nice," Oculura said with a chill to her voice.

"It looks as if you've added to your collection," I said, watching the eyeballs swirl around inside the jar.

Oculura nodded. "I have. I believe seeing things from different people's eyes broadens my perspective and makes me more open-minded. Here, these should do," she said, reaching into the jar. "They don't match, but the previous owners were both very fair minded."

After removing her eyes from the sockets, she popped

in the new ones and blinked. "It takes a moment for them to come into focus. Ah, that's better!"

Adara gasped and put her hand over her mouth. "I think I'll go find Eadric," she said, and hurried out the door.

I narrowed my eyes as I watched her go. Whatever she was up to, I knew I wasn't going to like it. "Do you have a bowl I might borrow?" I asked Oculura. "And some water, if you don't mind."

"Going to do some scrying?" Oculura asked as she fetched a pretty blue-and-green bowl.

I nodded and took the bowl from her hands. "I have some questions about Adara. She arrived at the castle, claiming to be a relative. I think she's up to something. Oh, thank you," I said as Oculura poured water into the bowl.

"So she's not a relative?" Oculura asked.

"Grandmother doesn't think so," I told her, and bent over the bowl.

I hadn't done much scrying, but I knew what to do. Passing my hand over the water, I thought about Adara. When the image of her face appeared in the water, I murmured, "Where does she come from?"

The image of a castle squatting in a muddy plain appeared in the bowl. It was an ugly castle with three low towers and very few windows. "That's Lower Mucksworthy," said Oculura. "Dyspepsia and I visited it once years ago. We didn't stay long, though. The stench from the mud flats gave my sister terrible headaches."

"Who is Adara's father?" I asked. Just because she came from a castle didn't mean that she was a princess. For all we knew, she could be a serving girl.

A moment later, a picture of a middle-aged man sitting on a throne appeared in the water. His arm was propped on the arm of the throne and he was resting his chin in his hand, watching children of various ages playing at his feet. The man looked weary, even in the wavery image.

"So her father is the king," I said. "Why did she come to Greater Greensward and what does she plan to do?"

The image of the king disappeared, and one showing Eadric's mother talking to Adara appeared in its place. I had never visited Upper Montevista, but I guessed that's where they were when I saw the mountains through a window.

With Oculura watching over my shoulder, I repeated my question. Nothing happened for a moment, so I leaned closer, concentrating harder. Suddenly the image became clearer and we could actually hear the muted voices of Queen Frazzela and Adara.

"You are lovely, my dear," said Frazzela. "You're just the kind of princess I had hoped my son Eadric would marry. Tell me, have you ever visited Greater Greensward?"

Adara shook her head. "No, I've never had the opportunity to go there. This is my first trip outside Lower Mucksworthy."

"I've always thought that was such an unfortunate name for a kingdom. Mucksworthy! Ah well, it can't be helped. I chose you for your beauty, not your kingdom. Now, I want you to travel to Greater Greensward, where my son is mooning over a girl who is totally inappropriate for him. When you see Eadric, smile at him, bat your eyelashes, do whatever it takes to get him interested in you and away from that dreadful Emma. Once you've lured him away, bring him back here. You'll have the most magnificent wedding that you can imagine, plus I'll send your father all that gold I promised him. Do you think you can handle that?"

"Of course," said Adara. "I'll have him here before the end of the month."

"Excellent!" said Frazzela. "My carriage is ready to take you and . . ."

They were still talking when I passed my hand over the bowl again and the image faded away.

"Wow! That was impressive!" declared Oculura. "You got sound! I've never been able to get sound when I scry. You *are* the most powerful witch in the kingdom! Of course, I knew that when you turned yourself into a dragon at the tournament. I can't wait to tell the other witches about this at the next council meeting!"

"At least I know what Adara's up to now," I said. I wasn't surprised; I was angry. It had never occurred to me that my future mother-in-law hated me so much! I knew it was because I was a witch, but that didn't make it hurt any less. "I'll tell Eadric when Adara isn't around. I don't want her to know that I'm aware of her plan, at least not yet. Please don't tell anyone what you heard just now."

"What about Dyspepsia? Can I tell her?" asked Oculura.

"Not for a few days," I said. "I don't want her to tell anyone, either. Thanks for letting me use your bowl. It's very pretty."

"Keep it!" she told me. "I have five more just like it. Dyspepsia gave me six of them for my last birthday. I don't know anyone who needs six scrying bowls!"

"Thanks!" I said, and tucked it in the cloth sack I carried.

I waited while Oculura filled the platter from a tray of pastries resting on the table. As soon as she emptied the tray, it refilled itself. "I bought that tray at the magic marketplace," Oculura explained. "After I bake something on it, the tray will refill itself up to ten times. I think I've emptied it three or four times so far today. I don't know how often Dyspepsia has been back in, but we should have more than enough for the entire rally."

"It's very nice of you to do this for Chervil," I told her.

"What are friends for?" said Oculura. "Have you talked to Dyspepsia yet?"

I shook my head. "We arrived only minutes before you found me."

"Then I'd better warn you. She's been getting hard of hearing lately, which makes her a bit grumpy."

Oh dear, I thought. Dyspepsia was almost always in a bad mood.

The first thing I saw when we stepped outside was Eadric carrying as many pastries as he could hold in two hands. When he saw me, he started walking in my direction. "Here, take the one on top," he said, holding up his hand. "They're really good! I've already eaten a dozen."

"He must have gotten those from Dyspepsia," Oculura said. "Maybe I *won't* have enough."

I took one and bit into it. The pastry went *poof* in my mouth and was gone, leaving behind a sweet and delicious aftertaste.

"They taste wonderful, but there's not a lot of substance," said Eadric. "I could eat these things all day and never feel full!"

"There's Dyspepsia!" cried Oculura. "I need to ask her how many times she's emptied the tray. I think I'll have to whip up another batch."

Eadric turned to me, a frown creasing his brow. "Are they running low?"

90

"Hello, Dyspepsia," I said as Oculura's sister approached. Dyspepsia's expression was always sour. She looked even more unhappy now, and grunted when I spoke.

"Why is everyone muttering?" she asked. "I see your lips moving, but I can barely hear you. Speak up!"

"It's not them!" Oculura shouted. "It's your ears. They aren't working like they used to! You should get new ones. I know! We'll start an ear collection for you—like I have my eye collection. Then you'd be able to hear all sorts of things!"

"I like that idea!" Dyspepsia replied. "What kind should I try first?"

The two witches had been shouting, so anyone at that end of the garden could hear their entire conversation. When Dyspepsia started to look around, half the fairies clapped their hands over their ears and hurried to the back garden.

"I guess Chervil is going to start his speech soon," shouted Dyspepsia. "Everyone is headed that way."

"Then we should go there, too!" Oculura shouted back at her.

Word must have spread about Dyspepsia's proposed collection, because more fairies covered their ears as she passed by. When we reached the back garden, we found it crowded with fairies big and small. I spotted Sumac, Maple, and Aspen with a group of other fairies who cared for trees. Maple waved when she saw me and looked as if she was going to come over until a rustle in the audience made everyone turn toward the podium set up next to a stone sundial.

Fairies stepped aside as a tall, thin fairy wearing a tunic made of slender leaves strode toward the podium. He had a pointy nose and sparse green hair, but the most distinctive things about him were the slugs following him across the garden. Some were ordinary garden slugs, others were much bigger. A few were almost the size of small dogs. When he reached the podium, the fairy turned to face his audience. He smiled and opened his mouth to speak, but suddenly glanced down and started to shake his leg.

Three slugs were trying to climb him. "Get off me!" he told them. "I can't play with you now. Can't you see that I'm busy?"

The slugs slid off, but the moment Chervil stood still again, they climbed back up. The fairy sighed and started to pace back and forth, leaving the slugs behind. Turning to the audience, he began his speech even while he walked. "Most of you know me, but for the few who don't, my name is Chervil and I'm hoping to become your next ruler. I know some of you have heard my opponents speak and . . . Ah, hello, Sumac. Hi, Poppy. I wasn't expecting to see you here today."

Sumac and Poppy smiled and waved to him, then turned to wave to the other fairies in the audience. When a ripple of applause spread through the fairies, Chervil scowled and cleared his throat. "Anyway, as I was saying, I'm afraid that I don't agree with either of my opponents. I think they both have bad ideas that would not work, no matter what they say. I propose that instead of antagonizing humans by banning them from the enchanted forest, or coddling them by using our gifts to do their work for them, we should remove ourselves from human affairs altogether. It is time we mind our own business and let humans mind theirs! Humans are violent and deceitful. They are going to bring themselves down! If we ally ourselves with them, we'll be brought down, too!"

"He's right!" shouted a fairy.

"Forget the humans!" cried another.

"Humans are always making stupid mistakes," Chervil continued. "I'm sure you've all heard the expression 'It's only human.' Everyone knows how foolish they can be. Well, I say we should let them make their mistakes!"

"What do you propose we do?" called Sumac.

"Cut off all ties with humans. Take our business elsewhere. Ignore them when they come to us for help. If you need help, ask a brother or sister fairy."

"But a lot of our friends are humans!" Poppy shouted.

"Then make new friends!" Chervil shouted back. "If

you have so many human friends, tell me this: Why have you turned your back on your fellow fairies?"

"I haven't!" Poppy replied, looking indignant. "I just—"

"What do we do when they come to cut down our trees?" shouted Sumac. "Are you saying we should let them?"

"Of course not!" replied Chervil. "We have others who can protect the forests. Let the ogres and trolls handle the humans. Support the Vili instead of scolding the poor women for protecting the forest animals by hunting down the hunters. The forest can take care of itself, if we only let it!"

"Are you saying we should let the trolls and ogres go wherever they want in the forest?" someone called out.

"I'm only saying that—" Chervil began.

I was horrified. From what Oculura had said about Chervil, I thought he would have been friendlier to humans.

"Queen Willow would never have agreed with this!" shouted a fairy with a puff of white hair. "She kept the trolls and ogres under control and never let them rampage through the forest."

"She was the wisest fairy ever!" yelled Maple. "None of the stuff that's been going on would have happened if she was around. Maybe we don't need a new ruler! We should wait and see if she comes back."

"Everyone knows that Queen Willow has been gone so long that she must have faded away!" cried Chervil. "She isn't coming back and she never designated anyone to carry on after her. Queen Willow's days are over, and it's time for change. We need a new ruler who can make wise decisions and lead us in the right direction."

"And you think you're that person?" called a fairy with a deeper voice.

"I most certainly do!" Chervil shouted.

"No, I am!" called out Sumac.

"No, it's me!" cried Poppy.

"How would you rule without a powerful magic wand like Queen Willow's? Do any of you have a wand like that?" called the fairy with the deep voice.

All three candidates shook their heads. "She took her wand with her," replied Sumac. "It's lost forever and there aren't any more like it around."

"Then what makes you think that you can rule?" the same fairy asked.

"Because somebody has to, and we have as much right as anyone!" shouted Chervil. The other two candidates nodded.

"And none of you are any good!" called someone from the other side of the garden. With that, the fairies began to leave.

Adara nudged me with her elbow. "That last fairy was

right. I wouldn't pick any of them. You're the Green Witch. Can't you help them figure out what to do?"

"I would if I could," I told her, "but I don't know what they should do, either."

Nine

When only a dozen or so fairies were left, the three candidates met by the podium. "You have a lot of nerve calling our ideas bad," Sumac told Chervil. "If anyone's ideas are bad, it's yours! You'd take us back to the dark ages, when trolls and ogres terrorized everyone in the enchanted forest! You talk like they're our friends, but they never were and they never will be!"

"They're better than humans, not including witches, of course," Chervil said, glancing at Oculura.

"Would anyone like more pastries?" the witch asked, offering the platter.

Everyone who hadn't left had gathered around the fairy candidates to listen to their conversation. Most of the audience were frowning, as if they didn't like what they'd heard.

"If you think that trolls and ogres are better than humans, you have a very short memory!" Maple cried.

"We've never had to go to war with humans, but our history is full of clashes with ogres and trolls. Queen Willow was the one who saved us from them, and now you want to undo everything she did!"

Dyspepsia sidled up to Aspen. "Has anyone ever told you that you have very nice ears?"

Aspen glanced at her and backed away.

"What would you have us do—coddle humans like Poppy wants us to?" Chervil shouted at Maple.

"At least humans don't torment us or toss us in their stew pots for flavoring!" said Poppy.

Chervil snorted. "Those are just stories made up to keep fairy children from straying!"

"That's not true!" shouted Poppy. "My grandfather 'strayed' into an ogre stew pot when I was only a few decades old. My grandmother has never smiled since and still hates ogres more than anything."

"You made that up!" Chervil declared.

"Are you calling my grandmother and me liars? Just because it didn't happen to anyone in your family doesn't make it untrue! You . . . you . . . rodent dropping!" shouted Poppy.

"If I'm a rodent dropping, you're snake spit!" Chervil declared, giving her a shove.

"Keep your filthy hands off my friend, you slug lover!" Sumac cried. Taking two steps forward, she punched Chervil so hard, he almost fell down.

"Stop it!" I yelled at them. "This isn't the way to solve disagreements."

"I didn't know that fairies acted like little children," Adara said, smirking.

I had to jump back as fairy magic shot past me. Suddenly the air was filled with sparkling lights as fairies shot magic from their wands and threw it with their fingers. It looked as if even some of the audience had joined in. Glowing balls of light cut through the air, hitting flowers, the cottage, and the podium, exploding in bright puffs of fairy dust.

Everyone ducked and wove, trying to avoid the magic. When I looked around, the flowers that had been dusted with magic had grown long fingers on the tips of their leaves and were poking and pinching one another. The cottage chimney had turned into a long nose and was exhaling smoke. I gasped when I saw that the podium had grown four rabbit's legs and was hopping straight for me. It was time to stop this before someone got hurt.

"That's enough!" I shouted as I stepped out of the podium's way. Unfortunately, everyone was either so busy throwing magic or trying to avoid it that no one seemed to hear me. I nodded and started some magic of my own.

Fairies who don't listen
Will not hear my voice.
Make my next words so loud
They won't have a choice.

Facing the three arguing fairies, I shouted, "STOP THIS RIGHT NOW!" The words boomed so loudly that leaves shivered all the way into the forest. There was no way anyone could have missed it.

The fairies stopped what they were doing, looking stunned. Oculura stared at me, her mouth opening and closing like a fish's.

"Wow!" Dyspepsia said, twiddling her fingers in her ears. "That was loud! I guess my hearing isn't as bad as I thought. Forget the ear collection. I'm going inside to have a nice cup of tea and some of those pastries!"

"No more fighting!" I said, my voice normal again. "Is everyone all right?"

I looked around, but no one appeared to be hurt. The magic didn't even seem to have changed anyone. I was relieved, because witches' magic isn't nearly as strong as fairies', so I couldn't have undone their mischief. It would have been up to them to change their victims back. From the scowls on their faces, I didn't think they'd want to.

"I'm leaving!" Chervil declared. "There's no point in arguing with idiots!" A moment later, he was tiny and darting off into the forest.

"I was still talking to him!" Poppy declared. She was tiny and had flown off before I could blink.

"Wait for me!" cried Sumac, taking off after them. Maple and Aspen left moments later.

"Would you look at that!" wailed Oculura. "That stupid podium is crushing my flowers!"

The podium was still hopping around the garden, leaving a path of squashed flowers behind it. Oculura pointed a finger at it, but all her spell did was cover the podium with blue feathers.

"I don't think that's going to work," I told her. "Fairy magic has its own rules."

"I know," she said, "but I thought it was worth a try. I'll just have to get those fairies back here to undo the damage they've done! I wish I knew which one was responsible. I do know one thing, though. This is the last time I'll ever let a politician hold an event at my house! Pardon me, Emma. It was nice seeing you again!"

Oculura darted into the cottage. When she came out, she was carrying a battered old broom. Shaking her head at the sight of the hopping podium, she jumped on the broom and flew off into the forest.

"Maybe we should stay and clean up," I said to Eadric.

"I need to go," said one of the remaining fairies, and four more left as well.

"We could help out," Eadric said, surveying the damage. "Although Adara won't like it. That's funny. I don't see her anywhere."

"I didn't see her leave," I said as I looked around. "Adara! Are you there?"

"Maybe she went inside," said Eadric.

"I suppose it's possible, but I don't think that—Ow! Something bit my ankle!"

I looked down. A small brown mouse was gazing up at me.

"Adara, is that you?" I asked when it waved its paw.

I bent down to pick up the mouse. She started talking as soon as I held her in my hand. "It's about time you noticed me! I've been calling out to you for ages! One of those dumb fairies hit me with a spell! I was sure someone was going to step on me before you noticed that I was there! Turn me back! I don't want to be a mouse."

I forced myself not to smile. After all her plotting and scheming, Adara deserved to be turned into a mouse. And watching her try to take my beloved from me left me unable to scrounge up even an ounce of sympathy for the girl.

"I wish I could," I told her. "But it isn't up to me. A witch can't undo fairy magic. I'm not sure what to do. There's no telling which fairy cast the spell that did this. I'd have to hunt down all the fairies who were here, and even then the one who did it might not change you back."

"You shouldn't have come with us," Eadric said to her.

The little mouse's nose began to quiver and she burst into tears. I almost felt sorry for her.

There were only three fairies left in the garden. The one wearing a spiky purple hat and a tunic made of pointy leaves was taller than the other two. I noticed that they seemed to defer to him and watched as he walked up to me.

When he spoke, I realized that he was the fairy with the deep voice who had questioned Chervil. "Pardon me," he said. "I just want to apologize for the way my friends acted. Fairies don't usually behave like that, and I'm sorry they did it in front of an esteemed person like the Green Witch."

"You know who I am?" I asked.

"We all know who you are," he said with a smile. "My name is Nightshade, and these are my friends Oleander and Persimmon."

The two fairies smiled at me. The shorter one waved while the taller one said, "Hello!"

"My friends and I feel that the candidates behaved shamefully," Nightshade continued. "None of them deserve to be ruler."

"I'm afraid I have to agree with you," I told him. "Fairies deserve someone wiser. It's too bad Willow is gone. She was the queen you needed."

"I think the other fairies were wrong about Queen Willow," said Nightshade. "I think she might still be alive. It's true that she's been gone for quite some time, but that doesn't mean she's faded away. It's possible that we could find her and bring her back."

"You really think so?" I asked him. "That would solve everything!"

"It would indeed," said Nightshade. "I was planning to go look for her myself. We'd be honored if you'd accompany us."

"I'd love to, although I have to do something about our friend here," I said, showing him Adara the mouse, cupped in my hands. "It seems that some of that errant magic changed her."

"Then you really should help us find the queen," said Nightshade. "She's the strongest fairy in all of fairy history. Her magic can override every other fairy's. If anyone can change your friend back, it's Queen Willow."

"Then I guess we'll be going with you," I replied. "Do you have any idea where we should start?"

"Her home would be as good a place as any," said Nightshade.

"Then that's where we'll go first," I said, and turned to Eadric. "Are you all right with this?"

"If you're going, I'm going," he said.

"We'll follow you on my magic carpet," I told Nightshade. "The sooner we find Queen Willow, the better."

Ten

Although I was sure I'd visited every part of the enchanted forest, I was surprised when Nightshade led us to a place I'd never seen before. After passing through an unfamiliar grove of alder trees, we came upon a beautiful, secluded lake. Trees surrounded three sides of the lake, while a wildflower-filled meadow nestled against the other side. The only tree standing on that part of the shore was an ancient willow growing at the water's edge. Its heavy arching branches swept the ground and reached down to caress the water of the lake itself.

"The queen makes her home in that tree," Nightshade announced, pointing at the ancient willow. "I doubt she's there now, but it's worth a try."

I had tucked Adara in my pocket so I wouldn't lose her. She peeked out, twitching her little mousy nose. "The queen lives in a tree!" she exclaimed. "I thought it would be a palace made of crystal or gold. How disappointing!"

A moment later, she disappeared back into my pocket as if nothing there was worth seeing.

Nightshade and his friends looked around while Eadric followed me to the willow. Brushing the branches aside, I slipped under the arching canopy. The long, slender leaves filtered the light, giving the space a pale green glow. When I didn't see anyone, big or small, I called out, "Queen Willow! Are you here?"

I didn't really expect an answer, but before I could call out again, flickering lights descended from the upper reaches of the tree. Four tiny fairies fluttered around me, the lights from their wings bright spots of color in the green of the willow tree.

"Who are you? What are you doing here?" asked a fairy covered in curly leaves.

"I'm Emma the Green Witch," I told them. "I'm looking for your queen, Willow."

"So are we! Do you know where she is?" one of the fairies replied.

I sighed and shook my head. "No, that's why I'm looking for her. Who are you? Do you live around here?"

"Of course we live around here! We live in this very tree," a fairy wearing a dandelion-puff hat said, looking scornful.

A fairy with fluffy pink hair hurried to say, "We're the ladies of the queen's court. We keep the queen company when she's in residence."

"When did you see her last?" I asked.

"Oh, my. I'm not sure. I suppose it was after breakfast," said a fairy wearing a gown of blue petals.

"You saw her this morning," I said, excited that my search might be almost over.

"Of course not, silly! It was ever so long ago," declared the pink-haired fairy.

"How long ago, exactly?" I asked.

"I'm not sure. Ages and ages, I think."

"It was hot out, wasn't it? I seem to remember fanning my face with a leaf when we said good-bye," the fairy wearing the blue petals said.

"Did the queen tell you where she was going?" I said. "What did she say before she left?"

"When who left? Dandelion? She didn't leave. She's right there!"

I wasn't getting anywhere with the ladies of the court. After thanking them, I slipped out from under the willow branches and returned to the meadow. Nightshade and his friends were there, talking to some other small fairies. When I looked his way, Nightshade shook his head. Apparently he wasn't having any better luck.

I had thought that Eadric was right behind me when I first slipped under the willow branches. He hadn't joined me, however, making me wonder where he had gone. I looked around, finally spotting him at the edge of the lake. He was talking to someone in the water, but I couldn't see who it was. A moment later, Eadric bent down to take off his shoes. Curious, I started walking along the shoreline. Eadric was wading into the water when I realized that he was talking to a water nymph with long green hair.

"Eadric, stop!" I called, and started to run.

He turned toward me and waved.

"What are you doing?" I asked when I was close enough.

"This nice girl invited me to see her underwater palace," he replied. "I've never seen one under a lake before. She says that the water is much deeper than you'd think."

"Shame on you for lying like that!" I told the nymph.

"But it is quite deep," she told me, trying to look innocent.

"That's not what I mean, and you know it," I said. "Eadric, she's a water nymph, not a mermaid like our friend Coral. There is no palace under the lake. She's lying to get you in the water so she can drown you! That's what water nymphs do!"

"How do you know there's no palace?" Eadric asked, looking skeptical.

I glanced at the lake. The water seemed clear, but I couldn't really see more than a few feet below the surface. For all one could tell by looking at it, an entire city might lie only ten feet down.

"Look, I'll show you," I said, and hurriedly made up a spell.

Murky water
Become clear
So we can see
What's far and near.

It wasn't much of a spell, but it did the job. The water became as clear as crystal, revealing a rock-strewn bottom, a snapping turtle chasing a school of minnows, and not much else.

Eadric's eyes grew round as he gazed into the water. Shaking his head, he picked up his shoes and stalked back to the willow tree.

"My Eadric is a good person, but he's far too trusting," I told the nymph. "I'm surprised Queen Willow let you lure men to their doom right under her nose like this."

The nymph shrugged. "She didn't, but she's gone now. Who's to stop me from doing whatever I like?"

"I am," I said, starting to lose my temper. "I'm the Green Witch, and until there's a new fairy ruler, I guess it's up to me to keep people safe. Leave this lake and don't come back. And if I ever hear that you're lying to people like this again, I'll turn you into a minnow and introduce you to the snapping turtle I just saw. Do you understand?"

The nymph swallowed hard and nodded. "I understand. I'll just get my things," she said, and slipped back into the water.

"You know she'll be back before the week is up," Nightshade told me. He had walked over when I was talking to the nymph, but I hadn't noticed until now.

"I'm sure you're right," I replied. "That's just another reason why we need Willow back."

⚜

We were gathered by the magic carpet, trying to decide where to look next, when I noticed a woman dressed all in white coming toward us from the forest. Ignoring me and the three fairies, she strode straight to Eadric and stared him in the eyes. "Are you a hunter?" she demanded.

"Huh?" said Eadric.

"Are you here to hunt?" she asked, prodding his chest with one finger.

"No, he's not," I told her, knowing full well that he hunted every chance he got when we were at home. That wasn't in the enchanted forest, however, which was what the Vila really cared about. I'd never met a Vila before, but my aunt Grassina had told me about them. Protectors of the forest and the animals that lived there, Vili were known to hate hunters who dared enter their forests.

"If you're not here to hunt, why are you here?" the Vila asked us.

"We're looking for Queen Willow," I replied. "Have you seen her?"

"Of course I've seen her. I live here, don't I?" the Vila snapped.

"Let me rephrase that," I said. "When was the last time you saw her?"

"Let me think," said the Vila. "Oh, I remember! It was when the dragons were holding their Olympics. Queen Willow told me that she was on her way to watch the contests. She'd received a special invitation and was very excited. I didn't see her again after that. Oh, my! Do you think the dragons did something to her? Maybe they cooked her! Or maybe one of them stepped on her and squashed her flat. They might have covered up the incident so they wouldn't get in trouble!"

"I doubt very much that the dragons hurt the Fairy Queen," I told her. "But it does give us somewhere else to look. Thank you!"

"My pleasure," said the Vila before turning to Eadric. "Are you sure you're not a hunter? You look like one."

"We need to go," I said, and hustled Eadric to the magic carpet.

We were just getting on when a fairy landed on the grass beside me and became full-sized. He was the handsomest fairy I'd ever seen, which means a lot, considering that most fairies are very attractive. He had thick, dark brown hair, and eyes the color of cornflowers. Tall, with more defined muscles than most male fairies, he was enough to turn any girl's head. I heard a little gasp coming from my pocket, so I knew that Adara had seen him, too.

"I hear you're looking for Queen Willow," he said in a voice that would have made a minstrel proud.

"We are," I replied, aware that Eadric was glaring at the newcomer. "Most of the fairies seem to think she faded away, but we don't know that for certain. The fairies need her. We're hoping to find her and bring her back from wherever she's gone."

"Have you had any luck with your search so far?" he asked, glancing from me to Eadric to Nightshade and his friends.

"I told them about the Dragon Olympics!" said the Vila, who I'd thought had already gone. "I think a dragon might have eaten the queen." She smiled at him as if he was the best thing since the discovery of fire, but he didn't seem to notice.

"We're going to see the dragons next," I told the fairy. "I'm Emma the Green Witch, and this is my betrothed, Prince Eadric. Nightshade, Oleander, and Persimmon have been kind enough to help us look."

"I see," the fairy said, eyeing our companions. "Then perhaps I can be of assistance as well. I, too, am looking for Queen Willow. My name is Acorn, and I'm an old friend of the queen's."

I nodded, having already noticed that his tunic was made of overlapping oak leaves. "We'd be delighted to have you along," I said. "Nightshade, I'll lead the way this time. I know exactly where to go."

"I wouldn't have used the word *delighted*," Eadric whispered in my ear as we took our seats on the carpet. "You could have said, 'No thanks!'"

"Why?" I asked. "He said he's already looking for her and he's an old friend of hers. He might have the insight we need to actually find her."

"Maybe," grumbled Eadric. "But I don't like him!"

Eleven

I had visited the Purple Mountains twice before. The first time, Ralf had taken Eadric and me to see his grandfather Gargle Snort, the king of the fire-breathing dragons. The second time we had gone to the heart of the mountain to see the Dragon Olympics. That was over a year ago. The Olympics were held once a year, but we hadn't gone to this year's games.

We were flying toward the mountains when the wind carried the scent of boiled cabbage our way. "Do you smell that?" I asked Eadric. "That means someone is practicing."

Eadric nodded. We had learned that the fiery breath of dragons was real fire that smelled like boiled cabbage. The smoke that their fire created formed pink clouds that the wind could carry for miles. The smell was an especially good way to tell if a dragon was real or a magic-created illusion. If you saw a flaming dragon but couldn't smell boiled cabbage, some magic-wielder was probably trying to trick you. Smelling cabbage near the Purple Mountains meant that someone was practicing their flaming for the next Olympics. According to my dragon friends, contestants practiced there all year long.

Turning the carpet into a narrow valley rich with caves on either side, I spotted the one I wanted and landed in front of it. It was a large cave, but I knew that it narrowed in back to form a tunnel that led into the mountain. The tunnel could take you many places, one of which was King Gargle Snort's lair. Eadric knew what lay beyond, but I didn't know if the fairies did. I wasn't about to tell them, either. Ralf had shown great trust by taking us to his grandfather's lair. I wasn't about to betray that trust to anyone.

As I got off the carpet, I reached into my pocket and took out Adara the mouse. She squeaked in surprise but looked pleased when I handed her to Eadric. "I'll be going in alone and I can't take her with me," I said.

"Be careful," Eadric said, and leaned toward me for a kiss.

Nightshade had been peering into the cave. "What is this place?" he asked. "I thought we were going to the dragon's arena."

"This is one of the ways in," I told him. "We can't fly there. The heat from the volcano makes it too turbulent for my carpet and might singe your wings. Even if we could fly in, a racing dragon might run into us or someone's flame might cook us. Only dragons can safely enter the arena from above. This way is much safer, although it gets very

115

hot at the end, and it would be easy to get lost." If one stayed in the tunnel long enough, taking the turns that Ralf had shown us, it was possible to reach the arena.

"I don't like this," said Oleander. "This place reeks of dragon."

"We should all go with you," Nightshade told me. "It's dangerous in there."

"I'll be fine," I replied, and turned toward the cave.

"I know you said that you're the Green Witch," said Acorn. "But dragon fire can hurt witches, too."

I paused long enough to say, "It won't hurt me. I'm not just an ordinary witch. Wait here. This may take a while."

I had started into the cave when I heard the fairies talking to Eadric. "How can you let her go like that?" Acorn asked him. "Aren't you worried about her safety?"

"She's the only one who would be safe in there," Eadric told them. "Emma knows what she's doing."

"She must have some powerful magic," said Nightshade.

"Oh, she does. Believe me!" Eadric exclaimed.

If I'd known when we started out that morning that I'd be visiting the Purple Mountains, I would have brought the fire- and heat-proofing salve that Ralf had given me. Without it, there was only one way I could enter the arena or see the king without getting cooked. I would have to go in as a dragon.

It was common knowledge that fairies were afraid of

dragons. Perhaps it was because fairies feared that they would get cooked or eaten or stomped on. Or perhaps it was because it was rumored that fairy magic didn't work on dragons. Whatever the reason, I hadn't wanted to change in front of them. It was true that they might have heard that the Green Witch could turn into a dragon, but on the off chance that they hadn't, I didn't want to frighten them.

There was more than one tunnel leading from the back of the cave, but I found the one I wanted easily enough. It was one of the biggest tunnels and the smoothest. For centuries, enormous dragons had passed this way. Scales on their feet and bodies had rubbed the bumps and uneven edges off the stone walls, floor, and ceiling over the years.

My footsteps echoed as I walked through darkness so complete that I couldn't see my hands in front of my face. Even so, I walked far enough that I could no longer hear Eadric and the fairies before I started the transition. I stood still with my eyes closed while the change came over me. Turning into a dragon no longer hurt, nor did it take as long as it once did. If I tried to hurry it, however, the pain felt like it would rip me apart. When I finally opened my eyes, the tunnel didn't seem quite so dark or so big. I was now three times longer than my human height, and my senses were more acute.

I continued on, passing openings that would lead me in the wrong direction. Eventually, I noticed a glow up ahead. Phosphorescent lichen grew in parts of the tunnel, making it easier to see. I entered a huge cavern where crystalline flowers grew all around me and columns of multicolored rock rose from floor to ceiling. "I wish Eadric could see this!" I murmured as I paused to look around. We had been there once before, but we had been frogs then and saw things very differently.

I walked on, my head turning from side to side as I took in my surroundings. Soon I entered another tunnel, and another after that, taking different branches and offshoots, until I finally found the one that led me to a large chamber well lit with lichen.

Although the cavern was just as rich with color as some of the others I'd passed through, it wasn't from stone columns or crystalline flowers. Instead, huge piles of different-colored objects covered the floor, leaving just enough space for an enormous dragon to pass between. As I stepped into the cavern, my foot touched a golden chalice that had fallen from the nearby gold pile. The chalice spun to the side, clinking across the floor.

"Who's there!" roared a voice. What I'd thought was part of the gold pile stood up. King Gargle Snort stared in my direction, his rheumy eyes not quite focusing on me. His golden scales glittered as he took a step toward me, smoke escaping from his nostrils as his anger grew.

"It's me, Emma!" I told him. "Remember me? I'm Ralf's friend. I became a Dragon Friend at the last Olympics."

"Why would you be a Dragon Friend if you're a dragon?" he asked as smoke billowed around him.

"I can turn into a dragon now. I think it's because I am a Dragon Friend. My magic became stronger when I breathed in your concentrated smoke."

"I remember now!" the king said. "And you're a green dragon! I didn't know green dragons existed. My grandson had a friend who was looking for one once. His friend was a frog, if I recall. Turned out to be human. A good sort, even so."

I smiled. I was the one who had been looking for a green dragon to help end Haywood's otter spell. It was the reason Ralf had brought me to see his grandfather in the first place.

"You're here just in time," Gargle Snort announced. "My talons are too big and clumsy to pick up some of the more delicate things. I was going to ask Ralf to come by, but you'll do just fine. Here, put these parchments in that pile, then come see me. I have lots for you to do."

Ralf had told Eadric and me that his grandfather sorted his collections in various ways. Apparently he was still sorting them by color. I didn't mind helping him for a little while if he could answer some of my questions.

"I wanted to ask you something," I said as I picked up the parchments as carefully as I could. The parchments were old and crumbly and I didn't like moving them, but it was better than leaving them on the ground to be stepped on.

"Hmm," he said. "What's that?"

"Did you invite the Fairy Queen, Willow, to the Dragon Olympics?"

"Yes, I did," Gargle Snort replied. "Lovely woman, for a fairy. Very nice and thoughtful, too. Gave me a gift when she arrived. Now, where did I put that? It should be right over here! Tell me if you see a blue bottle of mermaid's tears lying around. Ah, here's the ruby necklace I found yesterday. Put it in that red pile, please."

As soon as I was finished with the necklace, the king had me take a pair of tiny silk slippers with tassels on the toes to the green pile. I was setting them down when I found a cluster of seemingly freshly picked green leaves tied together with a cord bearing the label LEAVES FROM THE TREE OF LIFE. I was examining them when Gargle Snort called to me again.

"These three phoenix feathers got stuck between my toes when I was working on the gold pile. Would you mind taking them back there for me?" he asked.

"I'd be happy to. You were telling me about the Fairy Queen?" I prompted.

"Ah, yes," said Gargle Snort as he set a feathered head-dress on a multicolored pile. "I like her. She's not as scatterbrained as some fairies. I thought she was having a great time. Then I got called away for a few minutes. When I came back, she was gone. As soon as you've finished putting the feathers in the gold pile, take this crystal rose to the white pile."

"Did the queen say anything about where she was going next?" I asked.

"No, why would she? I thought she was spending the whole day here. Why are you holding those feathers? Don't they go in the gold pile?"

I nodded and hurried off. It looked as if I wasn't going to learn any more from the king. After setting the feathers down, I took the crystal rose to the white pile, placing it on a lustrous white fur beside a pearl as large as a melon. The king was muttering to himself when I sidled to the cavern entrance.

"I have to go now," I told him. "It was good seeing you again."

The king looked at me and blinked. "Who are you? What are you doing here? I didn't say you could come in!"

"Oh, sorry! Then I'll be going," I said, and hurried down the tunnel.

Finding a route to the arena was easy from the lair of the Dragon King. All I had to do was find an opening where the air was hot enough to blister human skin. Although it felt comfortable to my scales, the tunnel was too hot for the lichen to grow, so I was walking in the dark once again.

The air grew even hotter as I approached the opening to the arena.

Eager to learn something useful, I entered the enormous, bowl-shaped arena and stopped, my gaze drawn to the sky overhead. At least twenty dragons were flying above me, performing loops and spirals as they practiced their synchronized flying routine. Another group was flying just below them, racing around and around in a big circle as a dragon on the ground kept track of their time. None of the dragons looked familiar to me.

It wasn't until I glanced down that I finally saw someone I knew. Ralf's mother, Flame Snorter, was practicing her flaming. I walked to the distance-marked lane, as much to watch as to get her attention. A beautiful and delicate-looking red dragon, she was most well-known for her ability to flame. It looked as if her flames were even longer now than they had been at the Dragon Olympics the year before.

She had just finished her set and was talking to another dragon when she saw me and turned my way. "I'm Emma, Ralf's friend," I began. "I can turn myself into a dragon now and—"

"I know!" cried Flame Snorter. "I heard what happened at that tournament. Congratulations! I think it's wonderful!"

"Did Grumble Belly tell you?" I asked. "I ran into him and Ralf earlier today and they didn't believe me at first."

Flame Snorter laughed and shook her head. "I haven't seen him since this morning. I told him about it ages ago, but he probably wasn't listening. I meant to come see you once I got a break in my training schedule. I'm so glad you came to visit!"

"Actually, I was hoping someone could answer some questions for me," I said. "Did you happen to see the Fairy Queen when she was here during the Olympics?"

"I saw her, but I didn't get a chance to talk to her. There was so much going on that day! You know, I do remember that the queen was talking to young Sky Runner over there when he was between races," she said, pointing toward the center of the arena where dragons were swimming laps in the pool of bubbling lava. "He's the blue dragon with the lighter blue crest. You might want to talk to him."

"I will," I told the dragoness. "Thank you so much! I'll see you again soon."

Flame Snorter was still waving good-bye when I started toward the lava. The last time I was there, I had stayed as far from the lava as possible. But then, the last time I was there, I'd been walking around as a frog and wasn't sure how long Ralf's special salve would hold out. This time the lava seemed enticing. Even if Flame Snorter hadn't suggested it, I probably would have gone over for a closer look.

The lava pool was nearly half the diameter of the arena. It was the reason that the Olympics were held in the Purple Mountains. Dragons loved lava and held as many events in the pool as possible. One of the most popular events was lava swimming, so Sky Runner wasn't the only one doing laps in the pool.

Floating rocks had been used to divide the pool into lanes, most of which were occupied. Few of the swimming dragons noticed me as I walked around the pool to stand at the end of Sky Runner's lane. It took him three more laps before he looked up and saw me standing there. When he did, he scowled and said, "What do you want?"

"I'm sorry to interrupt, but I was hoping to ask a few questions," I told him.

"Why should I talk to you? I don't even know you!" he said, glancing from me to the bubbling lava as if he couldn't wait to get back to it.

"I'm a friend of King Gargle Snort and his family," I said, hoping that would lend some weight to my request.

Sky Runner sighed. "Oh, all right," he replied, and turned to point at the empty lane next to him. "If you want to talk to me, you have to keep up. I'm here for practice, not conversation."

The dragon didn't wait for me to get in but started swimming down the lane again. Although the dragon part of me was excited about getting in the lava, the rest of me was terrified. Certain that I was about to feel searing pain, I tentatively dipped one foot into the lava. To my surprise, the heat felt wonderful. I slowly started to lower myself into the pool then, but my dragon side took over when I was up to my knees, and I slid in the rest of the way.

I sighed as the heat of the lava surrounded me. It was like coming in from a cold day to sit in front of a roaring fire with a hot cup of mulled wine. The lava warmed me inside and out, making me so comfortable that I sighed with relief. Closing my second set of eyelids, I sank beneath the surface and floated, reveling in the sensation.

I stayed submerged in the lava until I felt the pressure change as if someone was approaching. Raising my head just enough to see who it was, I started swimming when I saw that it was Sky Runner. He was coming back down the lane and would pass me by if I didn't try to catch up. We were swimming side by side when I was finally able to ask him a question.

"I heard you talked to the Fairy Queen when she was here for the Olympics," I began. "Do you remember what she said?"

"Sure! It's not often that I get to talk to fairy royalty," Sky Runner replied.

"What did you talk about?" I asked.

"Mostly the games," said Sky Runner. "What events I was in. What I do to get ready. You know, that kind of thing."

"How did the queen seem? Was she happy? Was she having fun?"

"Yeah, I think so," Sky Runner told me. "At least at the beginning. But then we were watching a young dragon named Tory in his first race. His parents were rooting him on, and suddenly the queen started looking sad. She didn't say much for a while, then she said good-bye and left."

"Did she mention where she was going?" I asked.

"Not that I can recall. Well, that's it," he said, stopping against the side of the pool. "I'm going to fly around the arena a few dozen times before I head for home. It'll be dark soon and I have to be back here early in the morning to start practicing again. Did you have any more questions?"

"No, that should do it. Thank you for your help," I told him, and heaved myself out of the pool.

Although the lava had relaxed me, it left me sluggish and tired when I got out. I didn't feel like finding my way all the way back through the tunnels, so I took to the air and flew past the dragons that were still practicing. The updraft from the heat of the lava nearly flipped me over, but I was able to climb above the jagged edges of the arena and head toward the valley where Eadric and the fairies were waiting. When I thought I was close, but not too close, I landed and turned back into my human self.

The sun was setting when I found Eadric asleep on the magic carpet. Adara was curled up into a tiny ball on his chest, and she lifted her head when she saw me approach.

"That took you long enough," she said accusingly.

"I'm sorry, but it had to be done," I told her even as I looked around. I spotted Acorn resting on a boulder just a short distance away, but I didn't see Nightshade or his friends. "Where are the others?"

"Shh!" Adara told me. "Don't wake Eadric! He needs his rest."

"Don't we all," I replied, yawning.

Eadric stirred and looked up at me.

"Do you know where Nightshade and his friends went?" I asked him.

"They left right after you did," he said, and sat up to look around. "Aren't they back yet? Look, there they are, just coming up the pass."

Three tiny lights flew through the gloom cast by the mountain, landing beside the carpet. Acorn got up to join us as the tiny fairies grew big again.

"You're back!" Nightshade said to me. "Any luck?"

"Not really," I replied, shaking my head. "I spoke to three different dragons. The Fairy Queen was here last month during the most recent Olympics, but she left early. Something happened that upset her, although no one knew what it was or where she went when she left."

"Then I learned more than you did," said Nightshade. "My friends and I went exploring and talked to some of the area residents. It seems that a local fairy talked to the queen after the Dragon Olympics. The queen told her that she was going to the border between Greater Greensward and Soggy Molvinia, although she didn't say why."

"Really?" I said. "Then that's where we'll go next. How fortunate that you met that fairy."

"Wasn't it, though?" Acorn said, giving Nightshade an odd look.

Twelve

I yawned again and glanced at Eadric. He was tired, too, and it was going to be a long flight to the border of Soggy Molvinia. Not knowing what we'd have to face there, I didn't want to arrive exhausted in the middle of the night.

"I think we should sleep before we start out," I told my companions.

Something grumbled in the tunnel and a puff of dust blew toward us. "Do you mind if we move away from here?" Persimmon said, looking nervous. "I don't want to wake up to a dragon stepping on me."

"We passed over a forest at the foot of the mountains. Why don't we spend the night there?" Eadric suggested.

"Good idea," I told him.

Eadric and I took our seats on the carpet. When he tried to hand Adara to me, she squeaked and ran up his sleeve.

"I guess she wants to stay with me," said Eadric.

I glanced at his sleeve and nodded. "That's fine, as long as I can see her. Get out of there, Adara, right this instant!"

The little mouse nose peeked out of the sleeve. A moment later, Adara crept out. "I wasn't going to stay in here, although it is nice and warm."

"Just stay where I can see you," I told her. "I'm sure you don't want to make me worry about you and lose my concentration while I'm flying the carpet."

"Why are you so worried about her?" asked Eadric. "I'll make sure she's all right."

"That wasn't what I meant," I said. "She may be a mouse now, but I still don't want her rooting around in your clothes!"

❧

The forest wasn't very far from the cave, and it didn't take us long to get there. Even so, it was nearly dark before we arrived and I had to follow the light of the fairies' wings to a clearing where a little stream ran cold and clear. The fairies grew to full size to help us gather wood for a fire and enough nuts and berries for a meager supper. Eadric refilled the water-skin that he had brought with him. Once the fire was started, I sat down on the carpet beside him.

We ate our meal by the glow of three witches' lights that I positioned over the carpet. Nightshade, Oleander, and Persimmon sat under a nearby tree, talking quietly among themselves. Adara sat next to Eadric's foot as she nibbled half a walnut. She didn't say much because she was too busy eating. Acorn had also joined Eadric and me on the carpet. I noticed that he wasn't touching the berries he'd chosen as he gazed off into the darkness. "How did you meet the queen?" I finally asked him.

"We've known each other for a very long time," he said. "We grew up together."

"Do you know why she might be unhappy?" I asked.

"I have a good idea," he replied, looking glum.

"What is it? Did something happen?" I said.

He wasn't able to meet my eyes when he said, "I think it's more about what didn't happen."

"I don't understand," I told him.

Acorn shook his head. "I don't want to talk about it."

"Fine," I told him. "But do you know anything that might help us find her?"

Acorn finally turned to look at me. "When I do, I'll make sure to let you know."

I watched as he got up and walked away. I may not have learned much, but I had the feeling that he really did care about Willow, and it wasn't just because she was a good queen.

Adara was scrubbing her whiskers with her paw when she turned to me and said, "I don't understand something. If you're a witch, why don't you just use a spell to find the Fairy Queen? I'm tired of going from one place to another when we don't know for sure where to find her."

"Fairies are very powerful," I told her. "Their magic isn't the same as witches'."

I thought about what she'd said, though. Scrying to learn the truth about Adara had worked better than I could have hoped. My magic had grown ever since I turned myself into a dragon. Maybe I *could* see what had become of the Fairy Queen. There was no reason I couldn't try.

Opening the sack I carried, I took out the bowl that Oculura had given to me. "What are you doing?" Eadric asked.

"Looking for the Fairy Queen," I replied.

Borrowing Eadric's water-skin, I poured water in the bowl until it was half-full. When the water grew still, I bent over the bowl and said, "Where is the Fairy Queen?"

I frowned, unsure of what I was seeing. For a moment it looked like pouring rain and lashing branches, until suddenly the picture was gone and all I could see was my own reflection. When I tried again, my reflection just stared back at me.

"It doesn't seem to be working," I said, glancing at Eadric.

The fairies had all gathered around as I tried to scry for Willow. "I don't think Willow wants to be found," said Acorn before he turned tiny and flew into a tree.

Nightshade seemed to want to say something, but instead he and his two friends turned tiny as well and found a tree of their own.

It looked as if all four fairies were wrapping themselves

in leaves for the night. Because fairies often spent their evenings dancing or visiting one another, I decided that they must be as tired as Eadric and I if they were going to sleep so early.

"We could sleep on the carpet, I suppose," Eadric said, rubbing his spine, "as long as we can find a spot without too many rocks. My back still hurts from sleeping on one earlier."

"We don't need to worry about rocks," I said. "Lie down and I'll show you."

Eadric looked skeptical when he stretched out on the carpet. Lying down beside him, I twitched my fingers and made us rise a foot above the ground. Floating in the air feels wonderful when you're lying down with nothing but an age-softened carpet and air beneath you. Before Eadric could say anything about being cold, I said,

> Whisper soft and kitten warm,
> Two blankets will be fine.
> Two pillows for beneath our heads,
> One's Eadric's and one's mine.

Eadric gasped when blankets suddenly covered us and pillows plumped under our heads. "This is great! We should camp like this more often!"

"So you like sleeping on a magic carpet?" I asked, smiling into the dark.

"I will now!" he said. "Imagine, no ants or spiders to crawl on us, plus it feels like we're floating on a cloud. Are you sure this will stay up all night?"

"Positive!" I said. "I have to concentrate only when I'm making it move."

"What if I fall off?" Adara asked from up by Eadric's head.

"You won't have far to fall, but you're small enough that you still might get hurt," I told her. "Don't move around and you'll be fine."

"That's easy enough for you to say," Adara grumbled. "You're not a mouse and frightened of every little sound."

"Then that shouldn't be a problem," said Eadric. "Haven't you noticed how quiet it is here? I don't even hear crickets chirping. Hey, look at the sky over the mountains! You can see the glow of the lava and the dragons' fire."

"And the outlines of flying dragons!" I said. "Some of them must practice at night. See, there's one now. If you look straight up, you'll see it flying above us."

"You know what you don't see?" asked Eadric. "The lights from the fairies who live around here. Normally fairy lights are all over a forest at night."

I sat up to look around. Eadric was right. The forest was dark and quiet; the only movement was the occasional dragon flying overhead and the leaves rustling in the light breeze that stirred the air. Unlike the forests we'd visited before, there were no twinkling lights zigzagging through the trees. "Perhaps it's because we're so close to the dragons," I said. "Maybe fairies don't like to live where dragons are always coming and going."

"Maybe," said Eadric. "But there must be some fairies around if Nightshade found one to talk to."

"That's true," I said, my eyelids suddenly too heavy to keep open.

When Eadric pulled me to his side, I rolled over to face him, pillowing my head on his chest.

"This is nice," he said, kissing the top of my head.

"Mmm," I murmured, snuggling closer. A moment later, I was asleep.

I woke the next morning to Acorn saying, "Wake up, sleepyheads! The sun is shining and we have a long way to go today. Here, have some apples. I found an apple tree and brought back breakfast."

"How thoughtful," I said even as Eadric groaned.

"Do I have to get up now or can I keep sleeping?" he asked, tugging his blanket up around his ears. "I'm already on the carpet."

I laughed as I got to my feet. "I guess it won't matter if you're awake or not. Stay where you are if you want. Just don't roll over and fall off when we're flying."

"I won't," he said, and was asleep again a moment later.

135

Not wanting to take any chances, I had the safety straps wrap around him so he couldn't roll off in his sleep. When I was sure he was secure, I chose one apple from Acorn's gift and put the rest in the cloth sack. A minute later, we were flying toward Soggy Molvinia. I had finished eating my apple before we were out of sight of the Purple Mountains.

❧

For most of our journey, I traveled in silence with Eadric asleep beside me and Adara curled against his back. The fairies flitted around the carpet, resting on it when they grew weary. I enjoyed watching the scenery pass under us as we flew east toward Soggy Molvinia. Vast forests melted into farmland where stone walls and hedgerows divided the fields, reminding me of pieced-together quilts.

Eventually the farms were farther apart. Soon there were none at all—just swamp grass and bogs with no signs of roads or people. I knew then that we had almost reached Soggy Molvinia, and it was time to start looking for Queen Willow. Only a few minutes later, the gentle breeze that had accompanied us most of the way became stronger. Our ride became bumpier then, and Eadric woke as rain began to fall. Grumbling, he sat up to look around, saying, "Where are we now?"

"The border is just ahead," I said. "I'm not sure how we'll find Queen Willow, though."

"Maybe the fairies can help with that," Eadric suggested.

I nodded. "Good idea. Nightshade! Acorn!" I called.

The fairies flew through the rain, looking wet and bedraggled when they reached the carpet. "Can you find the queen from here?" I asked.

"We can try," said Acorn.

"I'll talk to the others," said Nightshade. "This won't be easy, though."

The two fairies flew off, and I soon saw all four darting across the landscape. It wasn't long before Acorn came back. "I didn't see her, but I think she must be that way," he said, pointing south. "When I went in that direction, the rain got heavier. As soon as I turned around, it let up behind me."

"That could be a coincidence," said Eadric.

"Maybe," Acorn told him. "But it's the kind of thing Willow would do if she didn't want anyone to find her."

"It's worth a look," I said, and turned the carpet in that direction.

The rain had been steady, but as we flew south, it suddenly became much heavier. When I tried Acorn's experiment and turned around, the rain nearly stopped. I turned back and it instantly became a deluge.

"I think you're right," I called to Acorn. "She must be somewhere up ahead."

We flew on, but the storm only grew worse until it was impossible to see in any direction and the wind was trying to push us backward. Although I soon lost all sense of direction, I realized that as long as the wind was coming at us from directly ahead, we were going the right way. Twice we got turned around and the wind let up. Both times I turned us back so we were facing into the wind and kept going.

Eadric and I sat huddled together in the middle of the carpet with Adara crouched under the edge of my gown. The fairies had given up trying to take shelter under the carpet, and were under a fold of my gown as well. A particularly bad gust nearly flipped the carpet over and we almost fell off. I was starting to think that we might have to walk when suddenly the carpet shook as if something had hit it and took a nosedive, dumping us the last few feet. No one was hurt, including Adara, but when I tried to get the carpet to move, I couldn't even get it to wiggle.

Not only were we completely wet and miserable, we now had no choice but to walk. I picked up Adara and tucked her in my pocket. She shivered and snuggled against me, too wet and cold to complain that Eadric wasn't carrying her.

The fairies grew big then, unable to get anywhere in the rain when they were tiny. Leaving the carpet where it was, we started walking into the rain with our heads down and our shoulders hunched. We hadn't gone far when the rain let up altogether.

"Thank goodness!" Adara squeaked.

"You can say that again," Eadric said as he wrung out the hem of his tunic.

Thirteen

We turned to smile at each other, certain that the worst was behind us. And then the mosquitoes arrived. They settled on us like a gray, humming cloud, biting every inch of exposed skin. The insects buzzed in our ears and tried to get in our eyes and noses.

"Do you think Willow sent these mosquitoes, too?" I asked Acorn, instantly regretting it when the insects flew into my mouth. I spit, trying to get them out.

"Probably," he said, "if she was determined to keep everyone away." I knew he had gotten mosquitoes in his mouth, too, when he started spitting just like I had.

"Can you get rid of them with a spell?" Eadric asked, barely opening his lips.

Desperate, I covered my mouth with my hand before saying, "I can try, but I doubt it will work."

Saying the first thing that popped into my head, I recited:

Mosquitoes small, mosquitoes large
We don't want you near.
Fly away and make it fast.
Then stay away from here.

The irritating hum stopped suddenly. I was beginning to think that my spell had worked when another swarm descended on us, joining the first. The noise was louder than ever. Not only had my spell not worked, it had actually made our situation worse.

"I'm sorry I asked," Eadric said with his hand over his mouth. "No more spells, please!"

After that, we tried to walk with our eyes nearly closed, but it wasn't easy. Eadric took my hand so we could stay together, which meant that I had only one hand to brush away the mosquitoes. Each time I slapped my cheek, I squashed at least half a dozen. When I saw that my hand was red with my own blood, I wiped it on the skirt of my gown.

We went on and somehow the swarm of mosquitoes got thicker. With my eyes squeezed nearly shut, I couldn't see much of anything, and might not have noticed when Eadric suddenly disappeared if he hadn't been holding my hand.

"Eadric!" I shouted, and spat out more mosquitoes. Turning toward where he had just been standing, I nearly stumbled into the same hole that had swallowed him. I caught myself at the very edge and staggered back a step or two. Putting my hand over my mouth, I shouted, "Eadric, are you all right?"

"I'm down here!" he shouted back. "I fell in a hole, but I'm fine."

I crouched at the crumbling edge, careful not to get too close. "How deep is it?" I called to him.

"Not very, but I could use a hand up!"

Suddenly Acorn was there, reaching past me. Even as he pulled Eadric out of the hole, the mosquitoes vanished as quickly as they'd appeared.

"It was the weirdest thing," Eadric said when he was standing beside me again. "The ground was under me, then all of a sudden it wasn't. I've heard about that happening, but it's never happened to me before. I think that's called a *sinkhole*."

"Whatever it's called, I hope there aren't any more around here," I said, eyeing the ground in front of me.

"Wow! You have so many mosquito bites, you look as if you have the pox!" Eadric said when he finally looked at my face.

"So do you," I told him, and looked around. "So does everybody!"

"I hate mosquitoes!" said Nightshade, scratching the back of his hand.

Glimpsing movement out of the corner of my eye, I turned my head to get a better look. "Eadric, do you see what I'm seeing? Am I imagining it or is that a will-o'-the-wisp?"

Eadric turned as another hazy ball of light appeared. "You're right!" he said. "I've never seen one in the middle of the day before."

"Whatever you do, don't follow them!" I told him as more and more appeared.

Eadric gave me an exasperated look. "I know better than that! I wonder if they're trying to lead us to more sinkholes, or just away from the queen."

"Either way, we're going straight ahead regardless of what those things do!" I announced, as much to the will-o'-the-wisps as to my companions.

I was starting to get hungry, so I opened my sack and offered apples to Eadric and the fairies. When I peeked in my pocket at Adara, she was curled up with her tail wrapped around her nose, snoring gently.

We started walking again and the balls of light came closer. None of them stayed for long, however, when it looked as if we were about to walk right into them. They scattered then, and the next time I looked around, every one of them was gone.

"There's a lake ahead," Acorn came to tell me. "I don't know if we should go to the right or the left to get around it."

"This is taking too long," Nightshade grumbled, and gestured to the left. "We should go that way." When his friends gave him pointed looks, he shrugged and started walking.

"Why is that?" I asked him. "The ground looks equally wet on both sides."

"It's just a feeling I have," the fairy replied, and continued on with his friends trailing behind him.

"A feeling, huh?" said Acorn. He shook his head and turned back to me. "I was going to suggest we try some magic. There's a search spell I know that might work. I just had to get close enough to try it. After all we've been through, I think we must be getting pretty close."

"I'm not sure if you should use magic," I told him. "I tried a spell to get rid of the mosquitoes, but it just made them worse."

"This spell isn't like that," Acorn said as he pulled a wand from his sleeve. "It can't possibly hurt us." With a few muttered words and a wave of his hand, he sent a bolt of blue light speeding through the air. It went only a few yards, however, before it hit an invisible wall. There was a twanging sound and the bolt came back at us, although now it was green. Eadric, Acorn, and I dove for the ground. Even so, the bolt hit the three of us with such force that it blew us into the air, throwing us a few hundred feet.

"Emma, are you all right?" Eadric asked, bending over me.

"I'm fine," I said as he pulled me to my feet and hugged me.

Eadric turned to Acorn, saying, "I don't think using magic of any kind is a good idea right now."

Acorn was careful when he touched a place on his cheek that was already starting to swell. "I think I have to agree with you. Willow is doing her best to keep people away, and her best is very, very good."

"Do you hear that?" Eadric asked, tilting his head. "It sounds as if someone is shouting."

Acorn squinted into the distance. "It's one of Nightshade's friends. I think he's jumping up and down."

"He certainly looks agitated about something. Either they found the queen, or someone is in trouble," said Eadric.

"I'll go look," Acorn told us. Turning tiny, he beat his wings and rose into the air, only to be blown back the way we had come when a strong wind sprang up out of nowhere.

"I guess Willow doesn't care if they turn tiny, but she doesn't want them flying any closer to her," I said to Eadric. "It may be a while before we see Acorn again."

"Then it's up to us to see what's going on," said Eadric. "I'll tell you right now, I don't have a good feeling about this." After sharing a glance, we both started to run.

The land that surrounded the lake was marshy and riddled with puddles so that we splashed with every footstep.

Nightshade's friends were standing side by side with their backs to us while they looked down at something. It wasn't until we'd almost reached them that I realized there were only two figures when there should have been three.

"Where's . . . Nightshade?" Eadric huffed as we ran.

"Good . . . question," I panted back.

Oleander looked up and saw us. "Don't come any closer!" he said, holding up his hand. "There's quicksand and we can't tell where it starts and ends. Nightshade stepped in it."

"Have you used magic?" Eadric asked.

"Nightshade did," said Persimmon. "He tried really hard, but it just made him sink deeper."

"Then Willow must have put it there," I said.

Eadric nodded. "That's what I was thinking. We'll have to try something non-magical."

"I don't care what you do!" Nightshade shouted. "Just get me out of here!"

Eadric and I stepped closer to the fairies. When we spotted Nightshade, he was up to his chin in wet brown muck, with his arms floating on the surface. He was still struggling and sinking deeper by the second. "Hold still, or you'll go under soon," Eadric warned him.

"I could use my carpet if it still worked," I said.

Eadric was poking the ground with the toe of his shoe, trying to find where solid dirt ended and the quicksand began. "He didn't get far before he sank," he finally announced, pointing at the ground. "All we need is something he can hold on to, like a branch. I'd use Ferdy's scabbard, but it isn't long enough."

"I don't suppose anyone has a rope," I said, not really expecting that anyone did.

We all looked around, but there was nothing to see except flat land, water, and swamp grass. Eadric sighed. "There's no other way to do this," he said, and began to pull his tunic over his head.

"What are you doing?" I asked, afraid that he planned to go in the quicksand after Nightshade. Instead he began to twist his tunic into a thick coil, knotting it as he went.

"There's nothing else we can use to pull him out. This ought to be long enough. Nightshade, I'm going to toss this to you. Grab hold, and relax your body. Let yourself float."

I held my breath as Eadric tossed the end of his tunic. It took four tries before Nightshade had a good grip. Although Eadric tugged and pulled, the fairy didn't budge.

"Maybe if you make yourself small, Nightshade," I suggested. "There wouldn't be so much of you to pull out."

"Or I could end up stuck down where my feet are now!" said Nightshade.

"Let me help," Acorn said, coming up behind us.

"How far did the wind blow you?" I asked him.

"Back to that sinkhole. I ran from there, but those darned mosquitoes got me all over again," he said, rubbing fresh bites on his face.

"Here, take this," Eadric said, handing the end of the twisted shirt to Acorn.

The two of them pulled as hard as they could, but Nightshade didn't move an inch.

"This isn't working!" wailed Oleander. He and Persimmon were standing on the other side of Eadric, but neither of them had made any effort to help.

"Oh, never mind! I'll get small and see what happens!" grumbled Nightshade.

"Pull!" Eadric shouted as Nightshade turned tiny. They yanked and the fairy shot out of the muck and flew headlong into Oleander, knocking him to the ground.

A moment later, Nightshade was big again, standing beside his friend. Muck dripped from his clothes as he staggered to get his balance. Grimacing, Eadric wiped the muck off his tunic and put it back on.

"I want to go with Eadric!" Adara declared, peeking out of my pocket. "I'll feel a lot safer with him. Did you see how he rescued Nightshade?"

Sighing, I handed the little mouse over.

I was wondering how we were going to get around the quicksand, so I walked all the way to the edge of the lake.

There had to be solid ground between the two, or the muck would flow into the lake's water. Without a stick or anything else to use, I tested the ground with my foot and found that the boundary between the muck and the water's edge was only a few feet wide. It wasn't much, but it was enough for us to walk on.

"If we stay at the very edge of the lake, we should be able to get past the quicksand," I told Eadric.

He nodded. "Sounds like a plan. I'll go first. Grab me and pull me back if I start to sink."

"I think Nightshade should go first," said Persimmon.

"Not this time," Nightshade said, wiping dirt from his neck.

We walked single file, following Eadric around the edge of the lake. After walking for a few minutes, Acorn started testing the ground on the side of the path. "We're past the quicksand," he finally told us. "Just be careful in case there's more up ahead."

"I think there's something other than quicksand in front of us, but I don't know what it is," said Eadric. "There's a funny colored line crossing the ground. It starts somewhere to the left and goes all the way into the lake."

I hadn't noticed the line, but I had noticed something else. Up ahead, so far away that I almost couldn't see it, I thought I spotted something that didn't quite fit into the marshy landscape. "Look over there," I said. "Is that a tree?"

"There aren't any trees around here," Eadric began, but when he looked where I was pointing, his eyes grew big. "That wasn't there a minute ago!"

"Or at least you didn't see it," said Acorn. "If I'm not mistaken, that's a willow tree."

It was hard to make out what kind of tree it was because of the green haze that surrounded it, but the more I studied it, the more I was convinced that he was right. "It looks as if we've finally found Queen Willow. Now all we have to do is figure out how to get to her."

"This line has me worried," said Eadric. "Let's see what it does. Emma, do you still have an apple?"

"You can't possibly mean to eat now!" said Nightshade. "We've almost reached the queen!"

"Eadric knows what he's doing," I said as I took an apple from the sack.

"You have food?" Adara squeaked, poking her head out of Eadric's pocket. "Why didn't you tell me? I'm starving!"

"First things first," said Eadric. Pulling his arm back, he flung the apple over the line. Light flashed and the apple fell to the ground as a hard, gray rock.

"It turns things into stone!" cried Oleander.

"I bet the line makes a big circle around the tree," said Acorn.

"We'll never get to Queen Willow now!" cried Persimmon.

Although Persimmon and Oleander both looked distressed, I thought it was curious that Nightshade didn't. He was watching me expectantly, almost as if he still thought I was going to do something. When I didn't, he took me by the arm, saying, "Emma, may I speak with you?"

Eadric was talking to the other fairies, trying to figure out something else they could do, when Nightshade led me away from them. Nightshade stopped and glanced back as if to make sure that no one could hear him before saying, "I had a feeling that you didn't want the others to know, but I've heard a rumor that you can turn into a dragon. If that's true, you should do it now. It's the only way we'll reach Queen Willow."

"I would, but I don't think it would do any good," I told him. "I'd get turned into stone like that apple or tossed back to the sinkhole the way Acorn was when he tried to fly."

Nightshade shook his head. "If you were a dragon, her magic couldn't touch you. Dragon magic is stronger than fairy magic. It's the strongest magic around!"

I was stunned. "Really?" I said. "I didn't know that! Are you sure?"

"Of course I'm sure!" Nightshade said with a laugh. "Every fairy knows that."

"Then I have no choice," I said. "Step back. I don't want to knock you down when I take off."

The first time I'd changed into a dragon in front of people, I hadn't been sure that I could do it. Now I knew I could, but I could feel their eyes on me, making me self-conscious. Eadric had seen me change a number of times already, so I didn't mind that he was there, but strangers were a different story, not to mention the pesky Adara. I turned my back on them before I began.

Dragon hearing is very acute. Even while I was only partway turned, I could hear Adara's mousey gasp and Nightshade mutter under his breath, "Finally!"

Turning toward the willow tree, I spread my wings and beat them once, twice, rising into the air above my companions. I hadn't gone more than three of my own body lengths past the line when hail the size of Eadric's fist began to rain from the sky. It pummeled me, bouncing off my scales, sounding like a bucket of pebbles tossed at a window. I closed my inner eyelids and would have kept going if I hadn't heard Eadric and the others crying out in pain.

"Ow!" someone shouted.

"That really hurts!" cried another.

"My nothe!" wailed a third.

Swinging my head around to look behind me, I saw them crouched on the ground, their arms wrapped around their heads and necks to protect them. I might be all right, but my companions were not and I wasn't going to leave them behind to suffer. Dipping one wing, I turned around and flew back to land beside Eadric. The hail stopped the moment I crossed over the line. Apparently, my ability to turn into a dragon wasn't going to help us, either.

Fourteen

Turning back into my human self, I knelt beside Eadric and put my hand on his shoulder. "Are you all right?" I asked.

"Ow!" he cried. "Don't touch me anywhere. I feel like one big bruise! But I don't think anything is broken."

"I think my nothe ith broken," moaned Oleander.

I thought he might be right; the fairy had a bloody nose.

I sat down beside Eadric while the others complained about their aches and pains. Persimmon whined about his head hurting and showed me the bruises forming on his arms. Acorn didn't complain at all, although he was rubbing the back of his neck as if it hurt. Adara had been in Eadric's pocket when he crouched down, and she swore he had squashed her.

Nightshade had a cut on his forehead that was bleeding a lot, but I didn't have much sympathy for him when

I saw the way he was glaring at me. "Why didn't you keep going?" he asked.

"Because it would have kept hailing and I saw how much it was hurting all of you," I replied.

He snorted and shook his head. "At least then you would have reached the queen. As it is, we're stuck here with no way to reach her. Why don't you try again?"

"Because I don't want to risk it," I told him.

"There must be something we can do," said Eadric.

"Maybe we could dig a tunnel under the line," Oleander said.

"Or walk backward all the way to the queen's tree," suggested Persimmon.

Acorn stopped rubbing his neck and looked up. "We don't know for sure that the line really does circle all the way around the tree," he said. "Maybe we should walk along it to see how far it goes or if there's a gap somewhere."

"A snake!" Adara squeaked, and ran up my arm. A long, brown-striped snake had stopped in the grass to look at us. We all watched as it started moving again, slithering across the swamp grass we'd flattened. When the snake slithered across the line, I held my breath to see what would happen. Nothing did—no flash of light, no snake turning into stone.

"Maybe that's our solution," I said.

"Get a snake to take us across?" asked Persimmon.

I laughed and shook my head. "What I meant was, maybe we can cross the line, too, if we turn into the kinds of creatures that live around here."

"But we're not from around here," said Nightshade. "What if the line doesn't let us pass? Then we'll be turned to stone like the apple. I think we should test your theory first. Adara is already a mouse. Let's send her across and see what happens."

"Oh, no you don't!" cried Adara from inside my sleeve. "I'm not anyone's experiment! I'll bite the first one who tries to make me cross that line!"

"I'll go first," I said, getting to my feet. "It was my idea."

Eadric reached for my arm. "Emma, you can't! What would I do without you if you were actually turned to stone?"

"I'll be fine," I told him. "Nothing's going to happen to me. Wait here and I'll—"

"I guess it works!" said Nightshade.

While I'd been talking to Eadric, Acorn had turned himself into a mouse and scurried across the line. When nothing happened to him, the others started talking about what they would become. Nightshade and his friends had just decided to turn into ravens when I set Adara on the ground. "Go with Acorn," I told her. "We'll meet you at the tree."

Turning to Eadric, I started to say, "I think we should become . . ."

"Frogs!" we said at the same time, and grinned.

Eadric and I had first met when he had been a frog due to a nasty witch's spell. He had convinced me to kiss him to turn him back, but I had turned into a frog as well. It had taken us a while to find out how to become human again. Although I'd hated being a frog at first, Eadric had taught me how to swim, hop, and catch insects like a frog. Being a frog had been frustrating at times and terrifying at others, but mostly it had been a lot of fun because of Eadric. Even now I had to smile when I remembered how enthusiastic he had been and how good he was at everything.

"Are you ready?" I asked him.

"Just a minute," he told me as he took off Ferdy's scabbard. "I don't know what would happen to Ferdy if I changed into a frog while I was wearing him. I don't want to mess up his magic."

"Good thinking," I told him.

Setting Ferdy on the ground, Eadric patted the sword, saying, "I'll come get you as soon as I can."

"*Now* are you ready?" I asked.

Eadric nodded. "This should be fun! I actually liked being a frog."

"So did I, most of the time," I said, taking his hand. Looking Eadric in the eyes, I recited an impromptu spell.

> Frogs we were
> And frogs we'll be.
> Make us frogs
> In one, two, three!

The instant I said *three*, the world seemed to grow huge around us. Eadric was still holding my hand, only now we had long green fingers that were smooth and slippery. I laughed when I saw the look of delight on his face. I'd forgotten how much he really did love this.

After giving his hand one last squeeze, I let go and started hopping toward the lake. Eadric's legs were longer than mine, so he landed in the water a heartbeat before me. The water felt wonderful, and I followed him to the bottom, reveling in the joy of being a frog once again. We chased each other for a minute, did somersaults, and twirled hand in hand before surfacing to bob on top of the water.

We were grinning at each other and treading water when I realized that this was the first time we'd been alone since we started to look for Willow. "I have to tell you something," I said. "I overheard Adara talking to herself at the rally. She mentioned your mother and how difficult something was, so I used a scrying bowl to see what she was talking about. Apparently, your mother sent Adara to Greater Greensward. Adara was supposed to win over your affections and take you back to Upper Montevista to get married!"

Eadric stopped moving his feet and sank beneath the surface. He came up spluttering, but I couldn't tell if it was from anger or from the water that had washed into his mouth. "My mother can never leave anything alone!" he declared when he could talk again. "She always has to stick her nose in my business! I'm not surprised that she sent Adara, just disappointed and mad that Mother would go so far! I suspected that something was up when Adara arrived in my parents' carriage."

"I didn't mean to upset you. I just thought you should know," I told him.

"And I'm glad you did. It's a lot easier to figure out what to do when you know the truth about something. Race you to the bottom and back before we start for the shore!"

"You're on!" I cried, and dove straight down.

Eadric won, of course, passing me on his way up while I was still swimming down. He was waiting for me when I reached the surface, and he pulled me into his arms before I could take my first breath. "You know I love you, Emma. There could never be anyone else for me," he said, and kissed me.

Although froggy lips are cold, their kisses are very nice. I enjoyed the kiss while it lasted, but all too soon we had to move apart.

"We need to go to the willow tree," Eadric said, his eyes still on mine.

"I know," I told him. "And we need to act more like real frogs and watch out for predators. We're just as vulnerable as any other frog."

"I'll keep us safe," he said. "But I have to say that being a frog with you was the most fun I've had in ages! I'll race you to the side by the tree."

"Ready, set, go!" I shouted, and started frog-kicking through the water.

We hadn't gone far when three shadows swooped toward us. "Watch out!" shouted Eadric, and we dove deep to wait until the shadows had moved on.

We swam underwater for a time, hiding in some water weeds when a big fish came close. Some tadpoles came to investigate us, giggling when Eadric made a funny face at them. As soon as we were able, we surfaced just long enough to look around and make sure we were still heading toward the willow. We were starting to go underwater again when a shadow appeared and Eadric yelped in surprise. I looked back and saw that a hawk had caught Eadric's foot with its beak and was about to carry him off.

"Oh, no you don't!" I shouted. With a thrust of my legs, I leaped out of the water and landed on the hawk's head. Grabbing a feather with both hands, I yanked as hard as I could. Startled, the hawk opened its bill, and Eadric plopped back into the water. I jumped off the bird's head and dove deep, searching for Eadric near the silt at the bottom of the lake. He finally found me and I hugged him so hard that he grunted.

"Thank you!" he told me, and gave me a big, froggy kiss. "You weren't acting very frog-like and I am so glad!"

"I wasn't about to let some old hawk steal my Eadric!" I said, and kissed him back.

We continued underwater after that. When we finally surfaced again, we had almost reached the shore and could see the tree just ahead. Three birds were circling the willow, cawing to one another. They looked oddly ruffled, as if they had been in a storm. It took me a moment to remember that Nightshade and his friends had chosen to be ravens.

Eadric and I were swimming to the water's edge when the ravens tried to land at the base of the willow. A sudden gust of wind blew them back, buffeting them so that they flipped head over tail, squawking. The wind didn't let up until the birds were back behind the line. When they had righted themselves, they drew together once again and started back to the tree.

The ravens were still circling the willow when Eadric and I climbed out of the water. "Nightshade doesn't seem to be having much luck," I said to Eadric. "I wonder how close we'll be able to get."

"There's only one way to tell," Eadric replied. "Hop to it!"

We hopped then, through the swamp grass, past a small turtle sunning itself, and around some prickly weeds. I froze when a shadow passed overhead, but it was just a wren, looking for something smaller than two good-sized frogs. We were approaching the willow tree when we heard something rustling in the grass. Eadric and I looked at each other, ready to flee, when two mice scurried out.

"Adara, Acorn, you made it!" Eadric cried.

"Now we just have to see how close we can get to the tree," I told them. "Nightshade and the others can't seem to get near it without being blown back to the line."

"We saw that," said Acorn. "But I noticed something else as well. Nightshade and his friends chose to be ravens, but the only birds I've seen who live around here are wrens, hawks, ducks, herons, and a pair of grebes. I asked a mole that we ran into if any ravens live around here. He said he'd never seen any until just now. I think Nightshade chose the wrong kind of bird. We might have better luck because we're animals that are more common."

"I am not common!" said Adara. "I'm a princess!"

"Right now you're a mouse," I told her. "And being common is often a good thing. If we're lucky, it will get us all the way to Queen Willow. Let's see if we can."

Acorn rose up on his hind legs and sniffed the air. "I don't smell anything that might eat us," he said. "Keep your eyes open, though. You never know what might be lurking in the grass."

While Acorn and Adara scurried from one clump of grass to another, Eadric and I took a more direct approach. We started hopping and didn't stop until we had reached the outer branches of the willow. Despite what Acorn had said, I half expected a strong wind to snatch us off the ground and blow us back to the line. It was both a relief and a surprise when we passed under the branches and could stop to look around.

"Where do you suppose we'll find the queen?" I asked Eadric as Acorn and Adara joined us.

"Right there," whispered Acorn.

I turned to where he was looking and gasped. A transparent chrysalis glowing pale green was attached to the tip of a branch dangling only a few feet away. Hopping closer, I almost tripped over a twisted stick from a curly willow branch that lay on the ground below it.

"Is that the queen?" Adara whispered.

I peered into the chrysalis and saw her. She was tiny, of course, and had long white hair that grew down past her feet. Other than that, I couldn't see her very well. She seemed sort of blurry and her features looked indistinct. When I looked really hard, I thought I could almost see

through her. I assumed it was what happened when someone was fading away.

"That's her," Acorn said with such longing in his voice
that I felt my heart flutter in response.

Fifteen

"Do you think the queen can hear us?" I asked Acorn.

"I don't know," he said. "I've never seen anyone who's actually in the process of fading away before."

"Let me see if I can get through to her," I told him, and leaned closer to the chrysalis. "Your Majesty, I'm Princess Emeralda, the Green Witch. I've been looking for you because the fairies need you. There's a lot of confusion because of your absence. The fairies plan to hold an election to replace you. There are three candidates, but none of them would make a good ruler; certainly not nearly as good as you. The things they have planned would destroy their relationships with humans. They've already caused fighting between the fairies."

When I didn't see any sort of response, I turned to Acorn and Eadric, saying, "I can't tell if she heard me or just doesn't care."

"Let me try," said Acorn. I stepped back and the fairy took my place. "Willow, if you can hear us, it's me, Acorn.

You probably remember me better as Oak. That was my name when you knew me. One day we were arguing and you said I should be named Acorn because I was so immature. A few years ago I decided that you were right, so I started calling myself Acorn until I felt that I was grown up enough to deserve you."

Acorn scratched his head and looked away as if trying to figure out what to say next. After clearing his throat, he started again. "I've always loved you. I guess I didn't say it enough, but it's true. Just recently I got my life in order and came looking for you, but you were gone and no one knew where you were. When I heard that you might have gone off to fade away, I thought my heart would break. I came looking for you to ask you to stay with us. I'm so sorry I never asked you to marry me. If you had, we would have had a child who would be your heir when you were ready to give up being queen. We could have gone off together and let your heir take over. Then none of this stuff with these bad candidates would have happened. I guess this whole mess is my fault and I'm really, really sorry."

"Look!" I whispered. "I think she heard you!"

A faint glow had appeared around the fading queen. It wasn't very bright, but it was a change.

"Keep going!" I told Acorn.

"Please forgive me!" he told the queen. "I should have wooed you while I had the chance. You were right to reject me when you did. I wasn't ready for marriage and you knew it. Looking back on it, I can't believe how much of my life I wasted when I could have been spending it with you. Please come back to me, Willow. I need you! We all need you!"

The light around the queen seemed to be getting brighter. She wasn't quite as transparent and I thought her features looked more distinct. Something was happening; I just hoped it was enough.

"If you come back now, I really hope you'll give me a chance to do what I should have done a long time ago," Acorn told her. "I know you used to dream about what our wedding would be like. My greatest wish is that you would let me make your dream come true."

"Isn't that sweet!" said a voice. "It's enough to make my stomach turn." A pointy-faced vole had appeared under the trailing branches of the willow. It took me a moment to recognize his voice as Nightshade's. When flying here as a raven hadn't worked, he must have decided that it was time to try another form.

Two smaller voles crept under the branches. His friends had made it as well.

"She hasn't faded away yet?" said Nightshade. "What a shame. I'd hoped she'd have it over with by now. When I was here before, she looked so close."

"What are you saying?" Acorn said, turning to face Nightshade. "Had you already found her?"

"Weeks ago!" Nightshade said with a laugh. "I was on my way home from visiting friends when I came across her. She was so far gone she didn't notice me, but she'd placed a powerful protection spell around herself that would keep working even while she faded away. It didn't activate until I reached for the wand. There it is on the ground, boys. Grab it!"

When I realized that the stick on the ground had to be the wand he was talking about, I jumped and picked it up. "Why do you want this, Nightshade? Could it be that you want the queen's power for yourself?"

"Give me that, Emma!" shouted Nightshade. "You have no use for it, and I need it. I'll make a better ruler than that old fairy or any of the others who say they deserve it. Give me the wand and I'll show the world what a fairy king can do."

When the two smaller voles lunged, snapping at my hands, I jerked the stick out of their reach and hopped away from the Fairy Queen. If we were going to argue over an old stick, I didn't want to put her in danger.

"If you knew where the queen was, why did you need me?" I asked Nightshade as he took a step toward me.

"Because when I reached for the wand when I was here before, her defenses blew me halfway across the kingdom. I was sure that the only one who could get close to her now had to be very powerful. The Green Witch with the power of a dragon was the best choice around. I was the one who told the fairies that the queen was fading away. I was the one who made them think about an election. I talked those three fools into campaigning, knowing that none of them could win. My friends put those campaign slogans in places that would upset fairies so that they would go to you for help. But you were too slow in coming! Eventually, I had my friends move on to a farmer's crops, knowing that was sure to draw you in. You finally showed up, but then I had to cast a spell on Adara, turning her into a mouse, so you'd have a personal reason to find the queen. And then I had to lead you from place to place. You never would have come here if I hadn't lied and said that a fairy had told me the queen planned to come to Soggy Molvinia."

I couldn't believe what I was hearing! "So this entire thing was a ploy to make me help you get the wand!"

Nightshade shrugged. "I did what I had to do. And to think that I put all that effort into getting you here, when all I really needed to do was turn myself into a rodent! If I'd known that, I could have saved myself a lot of trouble."

"You're the reason I came along!" Acorn told Nightshade. "I knew you couldn't be trusted, and I didn't want you to be the one to find Willow!"

"I don't know what you plan to do as king, but I'm not letting it happen," I told Nightshade.

"Don't be foolish, Emma. You have the wand, but I have something even more important to you."

I realized my mistake as soon as the words left his mouth. Nightshade, the nasty little vole, was going to use Eadric against me. I cried out as he lunged at Eadric and

169

bit down on his froggy arm only to drag him to the other side of the chrysalis.

Wrapping his front paw around Eadric's neck, he let go of Eadric's arm and shouted, "Give me the wand and you can have him back!"

"Don't give the wand to him!" Eadric hollered. "Emma, remember the hawk!"

In an instant I knew what Eadric wanted me to do. Shoving the stick in my mouth so that it stuck out both sides, I turned and jumped at Nightshade, landing on his head. He cried out and dropped Eadric, but instead of trying to get away, the vole grabbed hold of the wand and pulled. While I wrestled with Nightshade, Eadric bopped him on the head, trying to keep him from taking the wand. There was a *snap!* and the wand broke in two.

Nightshade groaned and backed away. "You broke it!" he cried. "Now it's no good to anyone! Do you know how much I could have helped fairies with that wand?"

"I know how much you could have helped yourself," I told him, wiping a piece of bark from my tongue. "I don't like being lied to or tricked. I won't forget this, Nightshade."

"Oh, I'm so scared!" cried the vole. "What are you going to do? You're just a frog!"

A strange look came into his eyes, and the next moment he and his friends were full-sized fairies looming over the rest of us. "Step on her!" Nightshade ordered his friends. "Quick, before she can change. And when you're done with her, step on old Queen Willow!"

I hopped away then, knowing how vulnerable I was as a frog. Oleander and Persimmon came after me, stomping and jumping as they tried to squash me. I made it harder for them by hopping between their legs. "Here I am!" I shouted. "No, I'm over here!"

I hopped back and forth so fast that they finally crashed into each other. While they untangled themselves, I hopped away from the chrysalis and the queen, knowing that I needed some space. I was going to change, but I wasn't going to be a human. Few things make me angrier than being lied to, although threatening to hurt Eadric was also at the top of my list. If Nightshade wanted a dragon, that was exactly what he was going to get.

Ever since I first learned how to turn into a dragon, I had practiced so much that I no longer needed to recite a spell. I started the change even as Nightshade and his friends came after me. "Uh-oh!" Persimmon said when he saw what I was doing. Grabbing Oleander's arm, he started to back away.

I was still close to the willow tree when Nightshade waved his own wand in my direction. While I completed the change, the willow branches whipped around me, pinning my limbs to my sides and tightening around my wings.

I roared as I reached full size. Stretching my wings and arching my back, I snapped the willow branches as if they were the thinnest of threads.

"You never said we'd have to face an angry dragon, Nightshade!" cried Persimmon. " Oleander and I are done here!"

Turning tiny, the two fairies darted off across the lake.

Not wanting to burn down the tree and the innocents still under it, I ran a few dozen yards and turned. Nightshade followed me, as I knew he would, but before I could take a deep breath, he turned the solid ground below me into quicksand just like the kind Eadric had helped him escape. I struggled, even though I knew that was the last thing I should do. The muck sucked me deeper, pulling me down until my legs and half my body was submerged.

Nightshade stood at the edge of the quicksand, laughing. "No one is going to be able to pull you out of that!" he shouted.

"No one needs to," I growled, and quit thrashing around. Taking a deep breath, I built up the fire in my belly and blew a long tongue of flame at the muck. Within seconds, the water in the quicksand began to boil.

Nightshade guessed what I was doing before I was half-done. When he raised his wand to point at me, I turned my flame in his direction. Yelping, he nearly tripped over his own feet trying to get away.

In less than a minute, I was able to climb out on the

now dry sand. In his hurry to escape my flame, Nightshade had dropped his wand and was trying to sneak back to get it. "You don't need that where you're going," I told him, and burned it to ash.

"No!" he cried, throwing his hands in front of his face as if he thought I was going to turn my flame on him.

"Don't worry, I'm not going to hurt you," I told him. "I'm taking you back to the fairies to tell them what you did. It's up to them to decide what to do with you."

"I'm not going anywhere with you!" Nightshade cried. A moment later, he was tiny and flying off in the same direction that his friends had gone.

"Huh!" I said, watching him go. "I guess he didn't need his wand for that."

Sixteen

The moment Nightshade was out of sight, I changed back into my human self and hurried to the tree. Eadric was still a frog, and I could see that he was holding the arm that the vole had bitten.

I cried out and fell to my knees beside him. "Are you all right?" I asked, reaching for his arm.

"I will be," he said. "As soon as you turn me back to my normal self."

I nodded and made up a spell as I went along:

> The frog I see before me now
> Is not his real form.
> Make him human once again
> Not cold-blooded, but warm.

By the time I got out of his way, he was already changing back. When he was human again, he flexed his arm. Smiling, he said, "Much better. It was a big bite when I was a frog, but now it's almost nothing. I'm not sure about that spell, though. It wasn't one of your best."

"I was in a hurry," I said, and kissed him.

"Emma, Eadric! Come quick!" called Adara. "Something is happening."

The chrysalis was glowing bright green now, casting its light on the faces of the two mice standing close to it. Eadric and I hurried to join them and got there just as the chrysalis split down the middle and Queen Willow sat up. Before she could climb out, Acorn had turned back into a tiny fairy and was reaching in to help her.

Although she looked like the elderly fairy I remembered from when I went back in time, a change came over her as Acorn took her hands and pulled her from the chrysalis. The wrinkles that had lined her face, neck, and hands vanished, leaving her skin as smooth as my own. Her long hair took on a greenish tinge until it was the color of willow leaves in the spring, and the leaves of her gown now looked fresh and supple. Even her movements changed, becoming easier and more fluid.

"Will you ever forgive me?" Acorn asked as he pulled her close.

"I already have," she whispered, and went into his arms. "I promised myself that I'd wait for you, but after the decades passed I finally gave up. I need you, too, Acorn! If you truly want the life you spoke of, I don't think I'll ever want to fade away."

"It's all I want now," Acorn murmured. "As long as it's with you."

Eadric shuffled his feet and looked away as the two fairies kissed. Adara scurried over to me and tugged on my hem. "What about me?" she asked. "I'm still a mouse!"

"This isn't the time," I told her, and smiled when Acorn and the queen turned to face us.

"Queen Willow, I'd like you to meet some friends of mine," said Acorn. "This is Princess Emeralda, the Green Witch, and her soon-to-be-husband, Prince Eadric of Upper Montevista."

"And I'm Princess Adara of Lower Mucksworthy," squeaked the mouse. "If you wouldn't mind, Your Majesty, do you think you could—"

"This isn't the right time," Eadric told Adara.

"I'm quite familiar with the Green Witches," Queen Willow said with a smile. "And I remember you, Emma."

I curtsied, and it felt odd to bend down to someone no bigger than my thumb. "I wasn't sure you would," I said. "I first saw you so long ago."

"I know," said the queen. "It was at Hazel's birthday party. I remember it as if it was just yesterday."

"Fairies have excellent memories," Acorn told me.

The queen nodded. "It's both a curse and a blessing that we rarely forget anything."

"I want to thank you for all you've done for my family," I told her. "Having the hereditary title of Green Witch

176

in the royal family has made a huge difference to Greater Greensward."

"It is I who need to thank you," said the queen. "I may not have looked it, but I was aware of everything that went on around me while I was in the chrysalis. I know what Nightshade tried to do, and I have all of you to thank for stopping him."

"You did say that the Green Witch has to ensure the safety of Greater Greensward's inhabitants, 'whether human- or fairy-kind,'" I reminded her.

"I did, didn't I?" she said with a laugh. "I guess fairies aren't the only ones with good memories."

"We should be getting back to the enchanted forest," said Acorn. "Who knows what's been going on there in our absence."

"Indeed," said the queen, and glanced at Eadric and me. "Are you able to fly?"

"We came on my magic carpet," I told her. "It stopped working back in the marsh."

"Then let me bring it to you," she said, and waved her hand in the air. There was a *whir* and a *whoosh* and my carpet hurtled through the air, slowing as it approached us until it landed gently on the ground behind me.

"How could you do that without your wand?" asked Eadric. "I thought you needed it to do magic."

Queen Willow laughed. "I haven't needed a wand since I was a child. Only fairies with weaker magic need wands to focus it. I carried that stick because of its sentimental value. It had no magical power of its own. My one true love gave it to me many years ago, didn't you?" she said glancing at Acorn.

"I found it and thought you'd like it," he said.

They were kissing again when Eadric turned to me. "I need to go get Ferdy before we start back, and I think we should go soon. It's getting dark and it will take us a while to reach your family's castle."

"I don't think we can go to the castle just yet," I told him. "There's something I want to do first."

When I glanced at Acorn and the queen, they were looking our way. "Would you like to join us on the carpet?" I asked them.

"We would love to go with you," the queen said, smiling. "I've never ridden on a magic carpet before."

"Good!" said Acorn. "That will give me time to tell you about the fairies who thought they could replace you. You won't believe some of the changes they proposed!"

"Is now a good time?" Adara asked as I picked her up.

"Not yet," I said, and tucked her in my pocket.

❦

Darkness fell as we flew over Greater Greensward, and the stars made the perfect backdrop for everything we needed to discuss. Acorn and Willow had grown to full size, so we could hear them over the whistling of the wind. When

Adara said that she was hungry, Queen Willow waved her hand to produce a loaf of bread and a large block of cheese. We all had our share, but Adara ate until her little belly was rounded and she fell asleep in the Fairy Queen's lap.

It was just past dawn when we reached the clearing where Oculura and Dyspepsia lived. Smoke drifted from the chimney and I could smell the tempting aroma of something baking. As we landed outside their garden, we saw Oculura scattering feed for her chickens. Eadric and I stepped off the carpet and started toward the cottage while Willow and Acorn stayed behind to talk.

The moment Oculura saw us, she came running. "Emma! Eadric! Is that you? Is everything all right?" she cried.

"We're fine," I told her.

"Thank goodness! We were worried that something might have happened to you when you left after that rally. There has been so much fighting the last few days! Fairies fighting fairies, friends fighting friends, neighbors fighting neighbors. It's been just awful. Why, yesterday two fairies started throwing rabbit pox pellets at each other right over our cottage. We had to chase them off and use the most powerful warding spell we had to keep from getting sick. They didn't get you, did they? You and Eadric look like you have the pox."

I reached up to touch my face. Somehow I'd forgotten the bites. They still itched, but not as much as they had at first. "No," I said, shaking my head. "The bumps are just mosquito bites."

"I have a cure for that! My special lotion will have them cleared up before you know it. Come inside and I'll get you some. You and your friends can join us for breakfast, if you're hungry," she said, squinting when she glanced back at Willow and Acorn. Apparently she had nearsighted eyes in today. "We were just about to sit down to fried apple cakes."

"The lotion would be great," I said.

"And so would the apple cakes!" added Eadric.

"I'm sorry to hear about the fighting," I told Oculura as we followed her to her cottage. "I might have a solution for that, but I'm going to need your help."

"Is it a new spell?" asked Oculura. "I'm very good with spell development."

"It's not a spell," I said, and glanced back at Willow and Acorn. "We'd like to call a meeting here at your cottage. All three candidates need to be here as well as any other fairies who would like to come."

Oculura shook her head. "I already told you that we don't ever want to help a politician again. The last time was a disaster."

"You wouldn't be helping the politicians," I told her. "But you would be helping fairy-kind. After this meeting, things should go back to normal."

"That would be wonderful! Now you *have* to tell me what you have in mind. Are you going to turn into a dragon and frighten them all into behaving themselves? That worked so well at your birthday tournament."

"Not at all. It will be something much better," I told her. *Although I will if I have to,* I added silently.

We had reached the cottage door and were just going inside when Dyspepsia looked up and saw us. She smiled when she noticed Eadric and me, but when her eyes traveled to the fairies who had finally caught up with us, she stumbled, almost dropping the platter of fried apple cakes she was carrying. Eadric noticed and ran to rescue them, helping himself to the cake on top as he set them on the table.

"Your Majesty!" Dyspepsia cried, curtsying.

"What are you doing, Dyspepsia?" asked her sister. "I know Emma is a princess, but we've never been formal with her before."

"Change your eyes, Oculura! Can't you see that Queen Willow just walked into our crumby little cottage?" Dyspepsia hurried to take the jar of eyeballs off a shelf.

Oculura looked puzzled. "And you say I'm the crazy one! You're imagining things again. Queen Willow has faded away. Everyone knows that! Oh, all right," she said, taking the jar when her sister shoved it at her. "These eyes are too nearsighted to be much good anyway. I put them in only so I could read the recipe for the apple cakes. These new recipe spells are tricky. You have to get them just right or you can have a terrible mess on your hands."

Oculura kept talking even as she fished around in the jar for two new eyes. "Not these. They don't fit quite right. And these see things only in a negative way. I want happy eyes today. Here, these will do. They're such a pretty blue, aren't they?" After taking out the old eyes and popping in the new, she turned and looked at Eadric and me. "My, those mosquito bites are terrible! And who is it you have with you . . ."

Oculura's jaw dropped when she finally saw her other guests. "You look like Queen Willow, only young. Is that what happens when you fade? Dyspepsia, maybe we should give fading a try."

"Be serious!" Dyspepsia told her. "That really is the queen. Welcome to our humble cottage, Your Majesty."

"Oh, right," Oculura said as she dropped into a curtsey. "Welcome, Your Majesty. May I ask what you're doing here? Or how you're young again? Or why you're carrying a mouse?"

"Sorry," I said, reaching for Adara. "I forgot you still had her."

"Is now the time?" asked Adara.

"Not yet," I told her. "Oculura, I can explain. Queen Willow is back with us because Acorn has been her true love for many years and—"

"It was true love's kiss, wasn't it?" cried Oculura. "I've heard that it's terribly powerful magic, but I've never experienced it for myself. Although I think I came close when Fred, the miller's son, took me behind the mill and—"

"Oculura!" said Dyspepsia. "The queen of the fairies doesn't want to hear about that. Although you can tell me the rest of the story later. I've never heard it before."

"I came back because Acorn is my true love and he needs me, as does everyone else, apparently," the queen said with a smile. "I'm sorry that there was so much chaos in my absence, but I believe Emma has a plan if you'd care to listen."

"Of course we'll listen!" exclaimed Dyspepsia. "At least I will. My sister never knows when to stop talking."

"Does anyone mind if I help myself to those fried apple cakes?" asked Eadric. "They're really very good."

"I want one, too!" Adara said, peeking out of my pocket. "Although I'd prefer a good piece of cheese."

"Let's all sit down and eat," said Oculura. "Your Majesty, you can sit at the head of the table and Acorn can sit next to you, if that's all right with you."

"That sounds wonderful," said the queen, leading the way to the table.

We were all hungry and the cakes were very good, so it took me a while to get around to telling the witches my plan. "It's simple, really," I said as I helped myself to another cake. "We want the candidates and as many other fairies as we can get to come to a meeting here in your garden. When they're all together, Queen Willow will appear to show them that she's back. They'll spread the word that she's here and that the fairies don't have to find a new ruler. One thing I learned from all this is how many fairies love you. They'll be thrilled that you're back and in charge, Your Majesty."

"And then our lives can return to normal!" declared Oculura. "I'll call everyone to the meeting right away! I can't wait to see their faces when they see you, Your Majesty!"

"Then you'd better make sure you still have the right eyes in," said Dyspepsia. "It would be a real shame to miss this!"

❧

The two witch sisters sent word of the meeting by singing bird, chirping cricket, croaking frog, and every other creature they thought could get the message out. While we waited for the fairies to arrive, Oculura slathered her lotion on Eadric, Acorn, and me. The itching from the mosquito bites stopped instantly and the swellings faded almost as quickly.

Fairies began to arrive a short time later, congregating in the garden under the watchful eyes of Oculura and Dyspepsia. Eadric and I were there as well, doing our best to keep any fights from starting.

Soon the garden was as crowded as it had been for the

rally. Most of the fairies I met knew who I was and were well-mannered when they saw me. Only a feisty fairy named Firethorn and an ill-tempered fairy named Thistle didn't seem to care that I was there. Firethorn had been declaring that he thought Chervil was the right candidate when Thistle told him, "Be quiet! No one wants to hear your opinion. Everyone knows that only dunderheads would vote for Chervil."

"Don't tell me to be quiet, you nincompoop!" shouted Firethorn. "My opinion is as good as anyone's, and certainly better than yours! Who are you going to vote for, that fool Poppy?"

"Poppy happens to be the best of all three!" Thistle shouted in Firethorn's face. "Close your mouth or I'll make you close it!"

"Oh, yeah! You and what army of ants?" Firethorn screamed back.

I started toward them when Thistle raised his wand and pointed it at Firethorn. "Maybe a spell to glue your mouth shut would give us all a little peace and quiet!"

"And maybe you should put that wand down before you do something you'll regret," I said, walking up to him. "This is supposed to be a peaceful meeting. No spell battles are allowed here."

Thistle turned and glared at me. "Oh, yeah? And how are you going to stop us? You're just a witch. Your magic won't work on fairies."

"I'm not *just* a witch," I said. "The rumors are true; I can be something else when I want to be. You really don't want to make me angry."

I decided that a show of strength might be a good idea, not only to stop the two fairies, but to deter any others who might be watching. Sometimes, frightening people can be the best option. I started to turn myself into a dragon. As I reached full size, the fairies started to back up, bumping into one another as they tried to get away from me.

"I won't hurt anyone who isn't here for a fight," I announced, and breathed a tongue of flame. "If you want to fight, leave now, and don't come back."

I swung my head around, meeting the eyes of one fairy after another. None of them spoke up, but none of them left, either.

The three candidates were the last to arrive. By then, the crowd was getting impatient and fidgety.

"Why are we here?" Chervil asked as soon as he landed and turned full-sized. "Is anyone in charge?"

"I am," I said, stepping forward. "In case anyone here doesn't know me, I'm the Green Witch and one of my duties is to watch out for the welfare of fairy-kind. I saw how you handled the queen's absence and I was very disappointed. None of the candidates running for your new ruler is good enough for you, so I decided to find one who is."

"What do you mean, not good enough?" demanded Chervil. "You won't find anyone better than me!"

"Or me!" shouted Poppy.

"Or me!" cried Sumac.

"Ah, but I did," I said, and turned to nod at Eadric. He hurried off and a moment later was back, ushering fairies out of the way as the queen swept through the garden with Acorn at her side.

A wave of sound broke over us as one fairy after another saw her. Although she was much younger than she'd been the last time she held court, it was obvious that she was the same fairy.

"Queen Willow is back!" they cried.

"Never fade, Queen Willow!"

None of the candidates spoke, but when a cheer went up, all three turned tiny and fled the garden. Queen Willow was indeed back, and everyone knew that she was in charge once again.

Eadric had come to join me. I changed back to my human form while cheers reverberated through the garden, the clearing, and even into the forest as the news spread.

"Now we can go home," I told Eadric over the noise.

"I can't hear you," he shouted back. "If you want to leave now, just nod."

I grinned and nodded. We ran to my magic carpet, the cheering of the fairies still ringing in our ears.

Glancing back as we took off, I saw Queen Willow and Acorn, standing hand in hand in front of her adoring crowd. Instead of facing the crowd, however, they were turned toward each other, sharing a look of true and undying love.

Seventeen

The moment we returned to my parents' castle, Grand-mother came running down the steps to the courtyard. I was still getting off my magic carpet when she said, "Emma, I have to talk to you. Where is that girl Adara? I thought she was with you."

"She's right here," I said, patting my pocket. Adara peeked out and blinked.

"A mouse, huh?" said Grandmother. "Good choice, although I would have turned her into a rat. Hand her over to Eadric. I want to talk to you without her listening in."

"I'll be right back," I said, passing Adara to Eadric.

❦

Grandmother and I walked only as far as the dovecote before we stopped to talk. "I found that information I told you about," she said. "Adara got one thing right: Ermingarde was married to King Snodgrass. She was his first wife, marrying him when they were both very young. She died childless a year later. I believe it was Mud Fever, which wasn't uncommon those days in damp places like Lower Mucksworthy. Snodgrass had five wives, but none of them gave him children until the last two. He was old by then and practically in his dotage. That girl doesn't have a drop of our blood in her and she knows it! Saying that she looks like Ermingarde! I knew she was lying the moment she said it!"

"I'm not surprised that we're unrelated," I told Grandmother. "Adara said something that made me wonder about her and Frazzela, so I scryed their meeting. This whole visit was a scheme they cooked up to get Eadric away from me."

"I had a feeling it was something like that!" Grandmother cried. "I don't know if you really want Frazzela as your mother-in-law, Emma!"

I sighed and shook my head. "I'm marrying Eadric, not his mother. I really want to like her, but she's making it very hard. Thank you for letting me know what you found out," I said, and kissed her cheek. "At least *my* relatives are wonderful!"

❧

When I joined Eadric in my tower room, Adara was sitting on my worktable, complaining. "Emma never let me ask

Queen Willow! Now I'll be stuck as a mouse for the rest of my life!" She saw me then and became even more agitated. "Until we left the garden, I thought it didn't matter that you hadn't let me ask her. I was sure you would ask her for me. But no, it was never the right time, and you were too *busy* to think about helping me!"

"I didn't need to ask her," I replied.

"Why, because you want me to stay a mouse forever so Eadric won't choose me?" asked Adara.

Eadric snorted. "Emma doesn't have to worry about that. I was never going to choose you for anything. Since the day Emma and I kissed and she turned into a frog like me, I've known that Emma is my true love. I would go anywhere and do anything for her. My life would be worthless if she wasn't in it."

"Oh, Eadric," I said, and stepped into his waiting arms.

We kissed then, but were interrupted when Adara whined, "Do you have to do this now?"

I pulled away reluctantly. Eadric touched my cheek, then glanced down when the mouse squeaked. Turning back to me, he said, "Do you have a piece of parchment that I could use? I need to write someone a note."

When I handed it to him, I was thinking so hard about what I was going to say to Adara that it didn't occur to me to ask about the note. As he walked toward my window seat, I looked at the mouse and said, "You must know that you never stood a chance with Eadric. He is the love of my life, too. It's time that you forgot him and found your own true love. I know you came here because Queen Frazzela sent you. I also know that you've been lying to us. We are not related in any way. If you continue to pursue Eadric, I will make sure that you remain a mouse for the rest of your life. However, if you promise to leave now, and never come near Eadric or me again, I'd be happy to turn you back myself."

"But I thought we either had to find the fairy who cast the spell or ask the Fairy Queen, who can fix anything," said Adara.

"We could have done that, but have you already forgotten that I can be a dragon? Dragon magic is even stronger than fairy magic. I could have turned you back at any time. I was just waiting until the moment was right."

"So is *this* the right time?" Adara asked me.

"It is if you make that promise. Remember, if you go back on your word, I can always turn you into a mouse again. Or maybe it will be something else, like a rat with mange or a squishy slug."

"I was going to make that promise anyway," said Adara. "I can't look at Eadric anymore without remembering what he looked like as a frog. I don't like frogs, and the thought of kissing one turns my stomach."

"And you'll leave right away?" I asked.

Adara sighed. "I promise to leave right away and never come back. Why would I stay? The people in this castle are crazy!"

"In that case . . ." Setting the little mouse on the floor, I said:

A human girl became a mouse
When a fairy spell was cast.
Return her to her normal shape;
The mouse form cannot last.

When nothing happened, it occurred to me that I needed to be a dragon, at least partway, for my magic to undo a fairy's. I started the change just enough to feel scales forming on my skin before I repeated the mouse-to-human spell. In an instant, Adara looked just as she had before Nightshade cast his spell. She was still as beautiful on the outside as she'd been before, but now that I knew what she was really like, I didn't see how anyone could think she was attractive.

"How should we send her home?" I asked Eadric. "I believe your mother's carriage is still here."

"Excellent!" said Eadric. "Then Adara can take this note to my mother. Get your things, Adara. Your ride will be leaving within the hour."

Beautiful Princess Adara twitched her nose and scurried from the room. I couldn't help but think that her movements were a little more furtive now—almost like a mouse's.

⚡

We had just reached the bottom of the stairs when I turned to Eadric and said, "May I ask, what did you tell your mother?"

"Here, I'll read it to you," he replied.

Dear Mother,

I know you mean me all the best, but you need to stop interfering in my life. I am going to marry Emma, my one true love, regardless of what you do or say. I knew what you were up to as soon as Adara arrived in your carriage. Really, Mother! Could you be more obvious? Trying to tempt me away from Emma by sending your hand-picked princess? It was never going to work!

Adara is a beautiful girl, but she is not for me. Neither Adara nor any other princess could ever compare to my Emma. I will never give Emma up for anyone, including you and Father. We will be getting married in a few weeks. If you and Father want to be part of my life, and that of my future children, you have to accept Emma and stop trying to break us up.

Your son (if you'll accept Emma),
Eadric

I couldn't stop grinning. "Wow! That says it all. You really didn't give her much choice. A few weeks, huh? Were you planning to talk to me about that?"

"Right now!" Eadric said, taking my hand. "Emma, will you marry me as soon as we can get it all arranged? A few weeks would do. Even sooner would be better."

Reaching up, I tugged his head close to mine and kissed him. "I would love to marry you as soon as possible," I told him after a long and lovely kiss. "Thank you for being you!"

"You're welcome?" he said as if unsure how to respond.

"I am so lucky!"

Eadric wore a goofy grin when he said, "Why is that?"

"Because I already know who my true love is, and I don't have to look for him or wait for him to come looking for me!"

❧

Eadric and I were watching the carriage roll away with Adara inside when Grassina joined us on the castle steps. "There's a rumor going around that you helped the Fairy Queen and have made all the fairies very happy. Would you please tell me what happened?" she asked.

"Nothing much," I said. "I reunited Willow with her true love, Acorn, and stopped a troublesome fairy from taking over. The queen is happy because she's about to enjoy the future she always wanted. Acorn is happy because he has Willow in his life. And the fairies are happy because the queen they love and respect is back. I learned a very important lesson from all of this, too. You should always believe in your one true love, even if it means you have to fight for him."

The start of a brand-new,
magical series by E. D. Baker!

Turn the page for a sneak peek.

The mood stone dangling from the gold chain around Aislin's neck glowed blue-gray against her sun-bronzed skin, but no one needed to look at it to know that the princess was worried. Only an hour before, the messenger had arrived with a summons from her grandparents, the king and queen of the fairies. King Carrigan and his warriors were about to leave for Fairengar, but Aislin still didn't know why. She'd returned to her room to fetch her good-luck charm so her father could take it with him, but so far, her search had been fruitless.

"Where is it?" Aislin cried, rifling through the clothes in the trunk by her door. The mirror on the stone mantel rattled as her agitation grew.

"What are you looking for, Princess?" asked a voice from the shadows. A doll, about ten inches tall, slipped off a small chair and pattered across the floor to tug at Aislin's hem. "Is there anything I can do?"

"A messenger told Father that his parents have summoned him and that he must leave right away," Aislin told her. "He's never received an urgent summons before, and I'm afraid something bad might be happening. I want to give Father my good luck charm to take with him, but he's leaving in a few minutes and I can't find it."

"I'm sure he'll be all right," the doll said, gazing up at the princess with amethyst eyes. A gift from the fairy queen, Twinket had quickly become one of Aislin's closest friends and was always there for her.

"I wish *I* could be sure!" Aislin cried. A tremor ran through the stone floor.

"Your father is a very powerful fairy," said the doll. "He can handle anything."

"So are my grandparents," said Aislin. "Which means there must be something terribly wrong if they need my father's help."

Twinket was startled when the floor began to shake in earnest, and she had to grab hold of a chair leg so that she wouldn't fall down.

There was one fairy quality that Aislin wished she *didn't* have—her temper. When combined with her pedrasi strength, her emotional reactions could be dangerous to others. This was the reason her two grandmothers had worked together to create the mood stone. When Aislin was an infant, the stone had helped her parents know why she was crying; even now, it was useful to warn people about her moods. No one wanted to be near Aislin when she was truly upset. She was so in tune with the rock that had been used to construct the castle that even the walls and floor shook in sympathy.

As hot tears stung her eyes, Aislin wiped them away with the back of her hand. Red eyes just wouldn't do! She had to say goodbye to her father, and he would see that she had been crying. The king had enough to worry about without worrying about her, too. Even a fairy as powerful as King Carrigan had to keep his wits about him when traveling all the way to Fairengar.

Aislin walked to a table, taking shuddering breaths and clenching her hands into fists while the floor continued to vibrate. "Are you all right?" Twinket asked, still holding onto the chair leg.

"I will be in a minute," Aislin replied as she poured water from a pitcher into a crystal bowl.

When Aislin was first old enough to understand her power, her grandparents had tried to teach her to control her emotions. When she turned four, she was still prone to lose her temper, so her pedrasi grandmother gave her the crystal bowl and showed her how to focus her energy and use it to calm herself. She learned that washing her face in the water from the bowl could soothe her anger. Everyone in the royal household was delighted when it worked.

The water felt cold as Aislin scooped it up with her hands, but it was just what she needed. Her agitation faded as she splashed water onto her face.

Twinket sighed with relief when the floor stopped shaking. "Let me help you find your good luck charm. It's small and green, isn't it?"

Aislin nodded. "The leprechauns gave it to me. It's a charmed emerald and—Wait, I think I know where it is!"

Running over to a table beside her bed, she opened the lid of a small box. "I found it!" she declared, and stuck the oval stone in her pocket.

There was a knock on the door. Aislin turned toward the sound. "Yes?" she called as the door opened.

"Your father is about to leave," an ogre footman named Skarly told her.

Aislin started running. "Thank you!" she called as she dashed past him out of the room and down the stairs. Passing a window, she heard the sound of the fairy knights' horses stomping impatiently in the courtyard. When she threw open the door, light from the torches lining the walls reflected off the silver armor of the fairy knights lined up behind her father's stallion, Wind Racer, nearly blinding her. She blinked, waiting for her eyes to recover. When she could see again, she spotted her mother, Queen Maylin, kissing her father while Timzy waited for his turn. Not wanting to miss saying goodbye, Aislin hurried down the stairs.

She had just reached her father's side when Wind Racer stomped his feet, forcing her to take a step back. She had been brought up riding the gentle ponies bred in the pedrasi mines, and while she admired the fairies' fiery-tempered horses, she had no desire to ride one herself.

Her father saw her and drew her in for a warm hug and a kiss on her cheek. Taking the charm from her pocket, she handed it to him, saying, "Please keep this with you for luck."

He smiled and patted her cheek. "I will," he vowed, tucking the stone into his own pocket.

A moment later, he'd mounted his horse and was raising his fist to signal that the troop was moving out. Aislin stepped aside as Wind Racer led the way over the cobblestones. Joining her mother and Timzy on the steps, she watched the fairy knights leave. Aislin counted them as they rode under the portcullis. Her father was taking all the knights stationed at the castle with him. That fact alone was enough to make her worry.

"Did you learn why Father was summoned?" Aislin asked when the last knight was out of sight and her mother had turned to go inside.

Queen Maylin nodded. "The messenger told us. Join me in my solar and we'll talk. It's time for Timzy to go to bed."

"But Mother . . . ," Timzy began.

"I let you stay up this late so you could say goodbye to your father," said the Queen. "You are not staying up any later."

By the time they'd sent Timzy to his room and had reached the queen's solar, Aislin was bursting with questions. A bright, cheery space with more windows than most, the solar was the princess's favorite room in the castle. There was no one there when they arrived, no ladies-in-waiting ready to cluster around the queen or minstrels ready to entertain her. Unlike the fairy royalty, pedrasi like Aislin's mother (and her grandmother, Queen Amethyst), didn't believe in royal formality in their everyday lives. Thankfully, this meant that the solar was one place where they wouldn't be interrupted; it was a good place to speak in private.

Mother and daughter headed toward the window seat, where they could see out over the forest. "You must tell me what the messenger said!" Aislin began.

"He told us that someone has been trying to open the northern passes and that humans had been spotted near the Magic Gate," said the queen.

"They can't open the Gate, can they?" asked Aislin, alarmed. "I was always told that Grandmother and Grandfather used the very best spells on it."

"It's true that humans can't open it, but the fact that anyone is there means something unusual is going on in the human lands."

"Please tell me all you know about the gate again," said Aislin.

Her mother gave her a tired smile. "When the fairies decided that it was time to leave the human lands, they came here to see my father. Once he gave them permission to make their home in the great forest, he helped your fairy grandparents, King Darinar and Queen Surinen, create the gate using enormous boulders and powerful warding spells. No one has been able to pass through that gate since. Only the eagles that fly high between the mountains are able to go to the human lands to report back to the fairy king and queen. Perhaps the eagles have seen something, but we won't know anything more until your father comes home to tell us."

"I hope he comes back soon," Aislin said, turning to look out the window at the darkened forest.

"So do I," said her mother. "More than I can say."

Everyone in the castle was used to seeing Twinket accompany Aislin on her excursions out of the castle into the surrounding forest. The day after the king left, she joined Aislin, Poppy, and their friend Bim as they headed out to go mushroom hunting. Twinket rode in Aislin's basket while Bim rode in Poppy's.

When the group reached the meadow beside Blue Lake, they spotted tiny fairies flying around with freshly picked mushroom caps on their heads. "Where did you find those?" Aislin asked one as she passed.

"I'll show you!" the fairy replied. "We heard you were coming, so we saved you some. There were oodles out here today."

Aislin knew all about mushrooms. When she was little, the fairies had taught her which ones were safe to eat and which ones she should never touch. Just because some were pretty didn't mean they weren't dangerous, and some of the most boring-looking mushrooms were the most delicious.

The fairy fluttered ahead, leading the way around the edge of the meadow to an ancient grove of oak trees. Mushrooms dotted the ground between the roots. As she drew closer, Aislin spotted more tiny fairies, peeking out from under their new mushroom caps, adjusting them so they fit just right. Seeing the princess, the fairies darted into the air in streaks of color, swirled around her long enough to say hello, and flew off into the woods.

Aislin and her companions were busy picking mushrooms when Timzy and his friends appeared, racing toward them from the far end of the meadow. The children laughed and shouted as they ran, and Aislin knew right away that they were playing one of her favorite childhood games—Magic Gate. It was a game in which "fairies" fled the "humans" until they had reached the magic gate; this time, it was a mulberry tree where someone had tied a scrap of red cloth.

The game was so popular in part because it was

based on something that had really happened in the fairies' history. For as long as anyone could remember, the fairies had lived side by side with the humans, trying to stay friendly, but avoiding involvement in their wars and conflicts. When distancing themselves became increasingly difficult, King Darinar and Queen Surinen decided that the fairies needed to move somewhere that the humans couldn't find them. The pedrasi king and queen, rulers of the land under the mountains, were happy to have them as neighbors. Once the fairies had moved to their new kingdom, the gate was sealed using powerful magic. Fairies and pedrasi can live for a very, very long time; hundreds of years had passed during which the fairies enjoyed their isolation and hoped that the humans would either forget them, or come to believe that fairies were a myth.

A pedrasi child screeched and ran past Aislin. The children looked as if they were having so much fun that Aislin was tempted to join them, and might have if she hadn't promised Cook that she'd bring back mushrooms.

Bim had no such reservations. "I'll play too!" the little sprite cried when he saw that other sprite children were playing.

"Aren't you going to collect mushrooms?" Poppy asked him.

Bim looked down at his empty basket, then at the mushrooms. With a twitch of his fingers, a mushroom flew into the air and landed in the basket. "Here," he said, handing the basket to Poppy. "I've done my share." With a wave of his hand, he scampered off to join the game.

Poppy glanced at the plum-sized basket. She sighed and shook her head. "One mushroom! I don't know why we invited him."

"Because he's our friend," said Aislin. "We always invite him."

The number of children living in the castle was growing. For a long time, fewer and fewer babies were born to pedrasi and fairies every year. Children were precious to both groups, but they were becoming increasingly rare. When the daughter of the pedrasi royalty married the son of the fairy royalty, the newlyweds kept their union secret until they learned that they were about to become parents themselves. Hearing that their children had married without permission, the pedrasi and fairy royal couples were furious, but nothing could have softened their hearts faster than the news of impending grandparenthood.

They gave the southern tip of the vast land between the mountains to the new parents, making them rulers of their own kingdom. King Carrigan named it Eliasind, a fairy word for strength. Now couples with children gravitated to Eliasind, where every sort of fey was welcome. Aislin had friends as tiny as six-inch tall Bim and as big as Igbert and Salianne, the giant brother and sister who lived with their parents in the deep woods. It wasn't unusual to find children of all sorts playing together.

Aislin looked up at a shout. The younger children were darting this way and that, trying to avoid their pursuers. Aislin's basket was half-filled when Timzy and five of his friends raced past, heading for the other end of the meadow. Two sprites and a little pedrasi child were chasing them, shouting, "You can't get away from humans!"

"Run, Timzy!" screamed Twinket.

Aislin grinned. With two sprites on the "human" team, the others didn't stand a chance. Sprites loved to cheat. Their motto was "whatever works." Then again, sprites weren't the only ones who didn't always follow the rules. Suddenly a troll appeared in the middle of the field, growling and slobbering and making the "human" children stop in their tracks. The glamour lasted only a few seconds before it faded away, leaving Peatie, one of Timzy's fairy friends, holding his stomach as he bent over, laughing.

Aislin and Poppy watched the children turn on Peatie and chase him around the field. Twinket tugged on Poppy's hem. "I think someone wants to talk to you," she said, and pointed into the woods.

A doe with soft, frightened-looking eyes was standing only a few yards away, pawing the ground nervously. Her speckled fawn stood behind her, its thin little legs shivering with fear. The doe made some high-pitched sounds that didn't mean anything to Aislin, but Poppy nodded and answered back.

"What did she say?" Aislin asked, irritated at the flash of jealousy that her friend could talk to animals while she couldn't.

"Tawny Coat says that there's danger in the woods and everyone must flee!"

"What kind of danger?" asked Aislin.

The fact that she had to wait for Poppy to ask the deer the question and wait even longer for a reply made her irritation grow. "People with weapons!" the fairy finally told her. "They hurt Sure Foot and the rest of the herd ran away. Tawny Coat thinks that the people are going to eat him!"

Aislin frowned. Neither fairies nor pedrasi killed or ate animals; they found the very idea repugnant. Whoever these people were, they weren't the normal kind of fey, if they were fey at all. "Where did she see them?" she asked Poppy.

"Near the big rocks in the pass," her friend eventually replied. "They don't look or smell like any creature she's ever seen before. She's going to warn the others." The doe and her fawn turned, their tails flicking as they bounded into the woods.

Aislin handed her basket to Poppy. "Please take the young ones and return to the castle. Tell my mother that there are hunters in the forest."

"Where are you going?" Poppy asked her.

"To learn more about them," Aislin said. "Father always says that you need to know the truth about something so you can make the right decisions. We won't know what to do until we know what we're facing."

E. D. BAKER is the author of the Tales of the Frog Princess series, the Wide-Awake Princess series, the Fairy-Tale Matchmaker series, the Magic Animal Rescue series, and many other delightful books for young readers, including *A Question of Magic*, *Fairy Wings*, and *Fairy Lies*. Her first book, *The Frog Princess*, was the inspiration for Disney's hit movie *The Princess and the Frog*. She lives with her family and their many animals in Maryland.

Visit her online at www.talesofedbaker.com.

Be sure to join the mailing list for book announcements and special giveaways!

Read the entire
Frog Princess
series!

Enter the magical world of
E. D. Baker!

www.talesofedbaker.com